Tales of Tears and Laughter

Tales
of
Tears
and
Laughter

SHORT FICTION
OF MEDIEVAL JAPAN

Translated by

Virginia Skord

HAWAI

University of Hawaii Press

Honolulu

© 1991 University of Hawaii Press
All rights reserved
Printed in the United States of America
91 93 94 95 96 97   5 4 3 2 1

Library of Congress Cataloging-in-Publication Data
Tales of tears and laughter : short fiction of Medieval Japan /
translated by Virginia Skord.
p.   cm.
Includes bibliographical references.
ISBN 0–8248–1315–4
1. Short stories, Japanese—Translations into English.
2. Japanese fiction—1185–1600—Translations into English.
3. Short stories, English—Translations from Japanese.
4. English fiction—Translations from Japanese.
I. Skord, Virginia S.
PL 782.E8T36   1991
895.6'3010802—dc20   90–27817
CIP

University of Hawaii Press books are printed
on acid-free paper and meet the guidelines
for permanence and durability of the Council
on Library Resources

Contents

v

Introduction

The stories in this collection constitute just a small portion of a vast body of some four hundred short narratives known as *otogi-zōshi*. Composed in the medieval period, roughly from the late twelfth through the early seventeenth centuries, these tales range from lyrical romances to ribald anecdotes, from pious accounts of divine beneficence to martial tales of vengeful warriors. They represent a cross section of medieval Japan in its richness and complexity, a panoply of life teeming with all the possibilities and contradictions of the age. Through these stories we can hear human voices speaking clearly across the centuries, telling tales of dismal failure and stellar success, of tears and laughter.

The irrepressible energy and constant flux of the times that produced otogi-zōshi are expressed in a graffito scribbled on a wall in Kyoto in the eighth month of 1334:

> Current fashions in the capital: attacks by night, burglary, forged edicts, prisoners, swift horses, brawls over nothing, freshly severed heads, apostate clergy and self-ordained holy men, overnight lords, lost wanderers, . . . monks mingling among the flatterers and slanderers at court, upstarts outdoing their betters, . . . swaggering warriors wearing court hats fashionably askew, crowds of rakes with lecherous intent prowling at nightfall, wives turning tricks under the guise of sightseeing, . . . starving horses, thin robes, old armor pawned and redeemed in installments, hick samurai off to work in palinquins, . . . archery contestants unable to pull their bows, tumbles from their steeds outnumbering arrows launched, . . . poetry parties everywhere, a world of open mayhem where everyone's a judge, . . . tea and incense competitions held even in the stronghold of warrior power, . . . loafing warriors throughout the city exchanging greetings on every street corner, . . . what a wonder that the country has been unified at all! Born in this imperial reign, you hear and see all sorts of amazing things. This is just a fraction of the chatter on the lips of the city's children.[1]

To the anonymous author of this graffito, this turbulence was cause for alarm, but the sword of reversal cut two ways. If to some the world seemed upside down, to others it was right side up at last. Given talent and training, a peasant could become a master of linked verse; given cunning and strength, a warrior could join the ranks of the military elite. Armed with the social lubricants of money and fame, practically anyone could rub elbows with the highest echelons of medieval society. In a periodically war-torn climate, the fortunes of aristocrat and warrior, clergy and peasant alike were liable to sudden drastic fluctuation. Misery and loss shared equal time with joy and plenty. Indeed, as the lampoonist says, it was a wonder that the country was unified at all; as it turned out, however, this apparent unification was but a brief lull. Years of relative peace throughout the courtly Heian period (794–1185) had been rudely shattered by the Genpei wars of the late twelfth century; the subsequent Kamakura shogunate had by the lampoonist's time dissolved into internecine disputes over dynastic succession. The fragile Ashikaga shogunate that eventually prevailed lasted little more than a century before it too was eclipsed by the devastation of the Ōnin wars (1467–1477). A further series of provincial wars engulfed the country in waves of turmoil and destruction that never fully subsided until early in the seventeenth century, when the Edo shogunate finally imposed upon Japan more than two centuries of peace and political continuity.

All of this tremendous upheaval might have unraveled the entire fabric of medieval society had it not been counterbalanced by an equally powerful force of reintegration, which allowed for a certain precarious stability. Rather than discard age-old values and social norms, medieval Japan reinterpreted them in light of new realities. Though the hereditary nobility may have fallen on hard times, neither their rank nor their traditional claim to cultural hegemony was ever discredited. Rich parvenus and rough country warriors in search of gentility looked to this aristocracy for models of deportment, their version of genteel behavior often at amusing variance from the model. Aesthetes discovered value in the rustic and humble, and the newly risen cult of tea drew adherents among plebeian and aristocratic circles alike. Sacrosanct religious tenets were scrutinized, inverted, even parodized, but never rejected; Japanese Buddhism was flexible enough to embrace apparent heresy into ever more sophisticated epistemological formulations. Similarly, in these otogi-zōshi, bumpkins marry into the aristocracy, renegade priests find an uneasy salvation in sin, mice struggle for survival in a world overrun by cats, wives chastise husbands, and lords are outwitted by their underlings. Yet through all this pandemonium courses a strong affirmation of traditional values and beliefs, ensuring that the society that emerged from the chaos was a reintegrated, revitalized continuation of the old.

The forces of upheaval and reintegration created a tremendous regenerative dynamic that permeated all aspects of medieval arts and led to an enduring cultural legacy. Much of what we now consider paradigmatic to Japanese culture—including the cult of tea, *nō* drama, linked verse, screen painting, landscape gardening, and the Japanese martial code—reached full flower in the medieval period. Among all the medieval arts, however, the literary tradition of otogi-zōshi has only just begun to receive the recognition it deserves. Unlike most Japanese arts, otogi-zōshi are as accessible to Western audiences as to Japanese. With their appealingly human context and entertaining narrative form, otogi-zōshi are easy to appreciate without reference to arcane aesthetic principles, historical processes, or religious doctrine.

We know little about the authors or the audience of otogi-zōshi. Facts are precious hard to come by and theories for the most part based on sheer educated guesswork; it is unlikely that these vexing questions will ever be resolved completely.[2] Only one story bears the name of an author, a man who is otherwise unknown to the literary world.[3] The most plausible reconstruction of their origins is best articulated by Barbara Ruch, who traces the tales to the medieval performance art of anonymous minstrels, itinerant preachers, and storytellers.[4] With their daily livelihoods dependent on the gratification (and subsequent loosening of purse strings) of the largest possible audience, these bards were obliged to create tales capable of evoking maximum emotional response within a mimimum of time. In doing so, they made use of themes and motifs near and dear to the hearts of their listeners, creating narratives with potential appeal for all segments of the population. Traditional folktales, legends, amusing anecdotes, historical incidents, didactic sermons, satiric gibes—all were fodder for these vocal artists. Not all the stories we now recognize as otogi-zōshi were actually composed by these minstrels, but the majority passed through performance media and were in some way influenced by it.

As Ruch points out, the composition and transmission of otogi-zōshi were but part of a larger vocal performance tradition that arose during the medieval period. Vocal performance was a literary rather than an oral art and was therefore dependent on a written text or libretto. In the case of otogi-zōshi, a performer might display an illustrated manuscript to an audience as he recited the stories with appropriate gestural and musical accompaniment. In the hands of professional storytellers, the tales once engaged visual and aural response in a variety of ways: the physical appearance and intonation of the narrator, gestural and pictorial illustrations, and the kinetic atmosphere of the performance site. If in the twentieth century we are unable to take part in the original performance, still we can clearly discern the vocal and performance element in the verbal text embedded in such devices as metrical regularity, formulaic phrasing, alliteration, and narratorial commentary.

Manuscripts of otogi-zōshi first appeared in illustrated scroll *(emaki)* format during the Kamakura period (1185–1333), when the emaki medium was at its zenith of popularity. From the early Heian period through the Edo period (ca. 1600–1868), the emaki was a commonly used medium for the transmission of a wide variety of artistic and literary subjects, of which otogi-zōshi constituted only a small portion. As the popularity of emaki began to wane toward the middle of the Muromachi period (1333–1573), otogi-zōshi increasingly appeared in short hand-illustrated booklets *(Nara ehon)*. Still later, in the early years of the Edo period, they appeared in printed picture books *(eiri kanpon)*. Although most otogi-zōshi were illustrated, they can be found unillustrated in either scroll or booklet form. To further complicate the issue, format itself was by no means fixed: it was not uncommon for scrolls to be cut up into booklets or, conversely, for booklets to be reassembled and their pages pasted together to form continuous scrolls.

The sheer number and kind of variant texts and physical formats in which the stories appear make investigating the development of otogi-zōshi a complicated matter. Any given otogi-zōshi text has undergone either a sudden or a gradual metamorphosis, depending on the number of times it was copied, what versions were lost and when, and the degree to which each copyist added his own anecdotes and interpretive commentary. A core plot often appears in many narrative versions in several physical formats, making most texts members of a genealogically complex family, the progenitor of which is not often easily identified. In cases where a number of texts of the same core story still survive, careful comparison can lead to a wealth of insight into the interpretive dynamics of this transmission process. Unfortunately, many early manuscripts are undated; of those that do bear a clear date, most are Edo period copies or retellings of earlier texts now lost. Many tales survived only because they were recopied later on, and we have no way of knowing the nature or number of manuscripts that did not make it through this winnowing process. The mere preservation of any given otogi-zōshi is more often than not random literary accident.

In the evolution of the content and physical text of otogi-zōshi, the scribe and illustrator played key roles. Since little more than rudimentary literacy was necessary to read or write most of the tales, the scribes may have come from an array of different classes or backgrounds, most likely from the ranks of townsmen, down-at-the-heels aristocrats, and lower-level and independent clerics. Such a copyist may have been revising a script for use as a performance libretto or transcribing a sermon that had impressed him. He might have been commissioned by another to copy down several tales so as to compile an anthology, in the process jumbling two stories together. He might have mistaken part of a manuscript for the whole and have been moved to flesh out the narrative from his own memory or imagination, as most likely the copyist of *The King of Farts* was obliged to do. He might simply have been engaged in writing practice, as was the imperial prince whose cipher appears at the end of *A Discretionary Tale.*

The illustrator made similar contributions to the evolution of the text. Aspects of the story not expressed within the text were often narrated graphically. Indeed, throughout the history of Japanese literature there runs a strong belief that "art provided direct access to profound truths which could be explained in words only with the greatest difficulty."[5] Not only are many otogi-zōshi amply illustrated, but those illustrations often contain supplemental captions providing additional dialogue, identification of characters, or explanation of scenes. In this way, the illustrations expand the referential world of the verbal text, inviting audience reaction and participation. Occasional illustrations depicting an audience and captions reporting excited comments on the event being narrated bring the audience itself into the story. Lacking the guidance of the storyteller, the solitary reader depended even more on textual illustration to form his interpretive response. Pictorial expression generally tended to conform to the nature of the tale itself: if courtly in nature, illustrations were sedate, revealing little individuality among characters; if scandalous or plebeian, characters were depicted in strong caricature. Even so, audience reception could still be significantly affected by the selection of scenes, composition, illustrative style and conventions, and the unique stamp of the individual artist.

Otogi-zōshi integrate elements of popular and canonical literary lore in often untidy bundles of cultural referents. Numerous literary precedents are represented within their narrative structure and content, testifying to the multiple strands of influence and tremendous variety of source material. Each story draws heavily from at least one, and more often several, preexisting literary genres or conventions, fusing them into new expressive combinations. The result will strike the reader as incongruous or innovative, ponderous or dynamic. In a pattern common to many otogi-zōshi, the rudimentary plot of a miracle tale, legend, or folktale is expanded through further detail or digression. Poetic allusion, citation of precedents or related tales, lists or catalogs of persons, places, or things relevant to the subject, and moralistic commentary on the action are just a few of the techniques of narrative expansion evident in these tales. The expansion of the popular Dōjōji legend into the long and detailed *Tale of Dōjōji* is accomplished through interweaving poetry and legends through the narrative as it progresses, resulting in a multilayered network of associations. The highly allusive and indirect lyrical style of classic Heian period prose fiction lends an aura of romance to the miracle tale *A Tale of Brief Slumbers*. In several stories, notably *Lazy Tarō* and *Old Lady Tokiwa*, casting an ostensibly serious tale in a humorous vein establishes two levels of reading, one according to the conventions of the parent genre and the other as a parodic undermining of that genre.

Like most literary products of medieval Japan, otogi-zōshi make frequent reference to a few paradigmatic classics, in particular, *The Tale of Genji*, *The Tales of Ise*, poetry of the famed *Kokinshū* and *Shinkokinshū* imperial anthologies, and the Chinese "Song of Unending Sorrow."[6] By the time otogi-zōshi were composed, not only had these works been valorized as enduring classics, but they had also worked their way into popular lore as sources of allusions, precedents, and poetic speechifying. In addition to these classics, quotations from and allusions to other poetry and prose, folktales, poetic commentaries, popular songs, aphorisms, and historical or pseudo-historical chronicles embellish the colorful narrative tapestry of otogi-zōshi. Much of the effect of *The Tale of the Brazier* is derived from the barrage of classical precedents and legends used to bring rhetorical weight to arguments advanced in a marital spat. Contemporary audiences must have roared with delight when they heard the worldy crone of *Old Lady Tokiwa* mix snippets of well-known songs into her litany of complaints and entreaties or the loutish young lady of *A Tale of Two Nursemaids* mangle the conventions of lyric poetry.

Chinese precedents were another ingredient of the pool of cultural referents used by otogi-zōshi composers. By the medieval period, the well-known Chinese aphorisms, legends, and didactic tales quoted in otogi-zōshi had become so thoroughly naturalized into common lore that they retained only the necessary hint of exoticism to ensure popular appeal and authority. It is for this reason that I have transcribed the Chinese names appearing in the texts in Japanese rather than Chinese pronunciation, rendering them consistent with a Japanese worldview.

By far the most revered of all the genres represented within otogi-zōshi was native lyric poetry *(waka),* traditionally esteemed by the Japanese as the most elevated of arts. By medieval times, trends within syncretic Buddhism and the long tradition of court-sponsored waka had culminated in the view that poetry constituted a supreme way of life by which the practitioner approached a higher level of spiritual consciousness. Consequently, poetic ability was considered the mark of the superior man; female worth and virtue were defined by a woman's poetic sensitivity. As is evident from *A Discretionary Tale* and *The Tale of the Brazier,* to charge that a woman had no appreciation of poetry was to pronounce a most damning indictment of her worth. Manipulation of the mystique of poetry could be a means to power, as in *The Tale of Ikago,* in which a provincial governor manipulates an underling's ignorance of poetry to try to wrest from him his beloved wife.

Poetry was also seen as possessing inherent powers to win over a prospective mate. Most otogi-zōshi passages dealing with love are richly adorned with poetry and poetic allusions. Descriptions of love are almost invariably expressed in poetic diction, and advances to the opposite sex are given weight by their allusions to poetry and famous poets of old. For Lazy Tarō and the little man, quick-witted extemporaneous poetry composition wins them the love of lofty ladies and universal respect. In *A Discretionary Tale,* a prospective lover seduces a faithful wife by reciting romances of the past. The poetic talents of these verbally adroit men are appropriate to the new age: whereas the classic romantic hero expressed a melancholy sensibility in languid and elegant verse, these assertive heroes are masters of verbal repartee and clever, if inelegant, verse. The success of their courtship lies in their adept appropriation of the traditional aristocratic domain of poetry and verbal wit. Thus, in the medieval world represented by otogi-zōshi, poetry had a practical, social, political, and even didactic function extending far beyond the purview of high-minded aesthetes who extolled its expressive power and beauty.

Otogi-zōshi have long suffered from what we would now call "bad press." Early in the eighteenth century, a small and not very representative sampling of the stories was published under the title *Otogi bunko* and advertised as appropriate reading material for women and children. Ever since, the public mind has identified otogi-zōshi with fairy and folktales. While it is true that certain supernatural events and beings derived from folklore have been featured in otogi-zōshi and that plots of certain traditional tales, such as the "Rip Van Winkle" *Urashima Tarō* and the "Tom Thumb" *Issun Bōshi,* have been retold in otogi-zōshi, this merely testifies to the wide scope of otogi-zōshi sources.

Once established, misperception became self-perpetuating, ensuring that those otogi-zōshi not conforming to the prevailing erroneus definition were dismissed as anomalies. The artless and occasionally even crude narrative style displayed by a few stories that were known did nothing to enhance the standing of the genre as a whole. As a result, the scholarly community labeled the stories a decadent form of earlier court-centered romances or inconsequential precursors to later developments in Japanese narrative,[7] valuable only as sources for stray bits of information on medieval life and culture. Yet recent years have brought an awakening of interest in otogi-zōshi as a literary genre worthy of serious attention.

Otogi-zōshi are almost invariably characterized as a genre, but the great variety within the corpus renders it stubbornly resistant to generic categorization. It seems that their medieval audiences never conceived of them as a distinct genre: the term *otogi-zōshi* itself (lit., "companion booklets" or "companion stories") is an anachronism. It was coined long after the stories ceased to appear, in a retrospective attempt to label short stories written in the medieval period. As it is currently used, *otogi-zōshi* encompasses a wide range of short prose fiction narratives composed in the medieval Japanese vernacular, tempered by influence from written canonical texts. For the most part, they are written in the native syllabic orthography *(kana),* as distinguished from Chinese or the mixed

Sino-Japanese hybrid known as *wakan konkōbun*. Given the lack of any systematic definition of Japanese narrative genres and their attributes, it is unlikely that a generic affiliation of otogi-zōshi, or even the question of whether the tales constitute a separate genre, can ever be satisfactorily determined. Ultimately, it may turn out to be more practical and theoretically appropriate to assign them to several different genres.

The role played by otogi-zōshi in Japanese literary history is a matter of some controversy. I see the tales as a synthesis of two historical Japanese prose forms, the *monogatari* and the *setsuwa*, which flourished in the Heian and early medieval times, then largely ceased to be produced. Generally speaking, monogatari are extended narratives divisible into books or chapters, relating either fictional or historical events. Setsuwa are brief accounts of incidents assumed to be true, normally compiled into larger anthologies. It may be more than sheer literary coincidence that both began to wane during the same period as the rise of otogi-zōshi, for otogi-zōshi incorporate significant features of both in a new narrative form. In length, otogi-zōshi are much longer than the average setsuwa but far shorter than the monogatari. Like monogatari, otogi-zōshi are whole unto themselves, whereas the setsuwa is usually read sandwiched between other setsuwa within an anthology. Otogi-zōshi feature the uncomplicated anecdotal plots typical of setsuwa yet, unlike setsuwa, explore the thoughts and motivations of characters more in the fashion of monogatari. Narratorial voice in otogi-zōshi ranges from overt, as in setsuwa, to covert, as in monogatari, sometimes shifting midway through the tale. Often we find an otogi-zōshi recounting several setsuwa-like stories in the course of telling another unrelated narrative or expanding a well-known setsuwa beyond its customary scope. In combining elements of both the setsuwa and the monogatari, otogi-zōshi created a new narrative form enhanced by the palimpsest of the old, generating means of expression that would be further developed in succeeding literary epochs.[8]

For a time, newly awakened enthusiasm for otogi-zōshi led to a flurry of experimentation with different classification systems in order to distinguish among the stories. Currently, the only widely recognized system is that devised by Ichiko Teiji, consisting of six categories (aristocrats, priests, warriors, commoners, foreign lands, and strange events and animals), each further divided into subcategories. This classification system, however, has the unfortunate effect of obscuring features held in common by disparate stories and of unduly emphasizing superficial resemblances between tales classified together. As literary phenomena, otogi-zōshi cut a wide swath across economic and social strata, blurring the boundaries of class structure. This is not to imply that all otogi-zōshi were cut of the same cloth. Many tales, notably love stories of the nobility and confession tales of priests, were written by and for a relatively narrow audience—the aristocrats and the clergy, respectively—and tend to be colored by the ethos and sensibility particular to these subjects. Even these stories, however, are not wholly contained by the narrow interests they appear to represent: they have a way of exuberently spilling over into the wider world, affording us a glimpse of life beyond the confines of the palace or monastery. It is this unique aspect of otogi-zōshi that is betrayed by classification schemes. No one has yet devised a system fluid enough to allow the application of multiple axes of reference that would permit easy recognition of their common features.

This collection, therefore, makes no claims to represent either the genre as a whole or any particular kind of story. In fact, a "representative collection of otogi-zōshi" implies a contradiction in terms—such an anthology would probably contain nearly as many stories as now exist in the entire corpus. I investigated many of the tales translated in this volume for my doctoral dissertation, which featured stories in Ichiko's "commoner" category. Examination of additional tales selected at random led me to realize the pitfalls of classification and to abandon further attempts at grouping (or, more properly, misgrouping). In selecting these particular stories for inclusion in this collection, I was guided by two criteria: variety of subject material and human interest sufficient to bridge the formidable barriers of time, culture, and language. I searched for tales that featured a variety of actors and that were universal in their scope and appeal. Most of the stories presented here are humorous, but not so consistently as to make humor their hallmark. Most contain generous doses of religious didacticism, but, given the paradigmatic nature of Buddhism in medieval Japan, the religious component is only to be expected. Most concern love and relations between the sexes, but what narrative about the human condition does not? If any thread binds them together, it is that they all express aspects of a common medieval Japanese sensibility as expressed by their anonymous authors and received by long-ago audiences.

Rendering the myriad nuances of Japanese literature into readable, engaging English is never an easy task, but translation of otogi-zōshi presents the additional challenge of recreating an entertaining story in English without destroying the conventions of the original text. I was obliged to set aside some fascinating stories because the degree of reworking necessary to present them effectively in English would have altered them beyond the acceptable limits of translation. As the reader will see, otogi-zōshi are not structured in the neat form essential to the successful Western short story. Rather, they are digressive and sprawling, often introducing elements that the Western reader might consider intrusive and extraneous. With the sole exception of *The Errand Woman,* which bears an uncanny resemblance to the modern short story, none of these tales displays a calculated gradual development to a neat, well-rounded conclusion. Instead, they seem to fade out, winding up with standard expressions of felicity and auspiciousness that will strike the modern reader as somewhat quaint.

I have resisted the temptation to rework a medieval Japanese tale as a modern short story, but in certain areas I have taken small liberties in order to maximize narrative continuity. A few overly long catalogs adding little to the flow of the story have been deleted, sentence order has occasionally been rearranged to accord with Western narrative logic, and captions and dialogue written into the illustrations have been integrated into the main narrative whenever possible or appropriate. All such editing has been described in the notes to each story. This attempt to give coherence to the tales may run the risk of compromising the impact of their original verbal and textual format, but, if any text is ill served by verbatim translation, otogi-zōshi would be rendered almost incoherent.

By far the most challenging aspect of this endeavor has been working with unannotated texts, the only format in which most of the tales are available. These texts have been transcribed into print from original printed or manuscript sources, with lacunae, corruptions, and miscopying preserved intact. In preparing the translations, it was necessary first to annotate the Japanese text: to parse the long strings of unpunctuated prose, supply Chinese characters where appropriate, identify possible textual errors, puzzle out lacunae, and track down allusions. Working with these texts has engendered a profound appreciation for those few annotated texts that are available and respect for the patience and erudition of their editors. I am grateful for the tremendous labor of transcription and compilation represented by the massive thirteen-volume collection *Muromachi jidai monogatari taisei,* which contains the printed texts of many of the stories translated here.[9] Were it not for this collection, most otogi-zōshi would remain locked in manuscript form, accessible only to those few experts able to decipher them.

Many modern Japanese textual transcriptions of otogi-zōshi present the stories solely as literary artifacts; conversely, good-quality photographic reproductions seldom legibly present the text adjacent to the illustrations. In divorcing illustration from text, the full impact of the tales is greatly diminished. This volume presents the written text accompanied by selected illustrations in order to give the modern English-speaking reader a sense of the literary and artistic effect experienced by earlier audiences of otogi-zōshi. I am grateful for the cooperation of the institutions who supplied photographs from the scrolls and picture books in their collections as well as permission to reproduce them.

Throughout the long process of selecting, reading, translating, revising, and editing texts, a number of people provided invaluable assistance. In particular, I would like to thank Karen Brazell for her careful reading of stories prepared for my dissertation, Tokuda Kazuo and Kasai Masaaki for their insight into medieval culture, Carolyn Haynes and John Mertz for their generous advice, and William Waters for moral support and late nights spent over countless drafts. A generous grant from the Japan-United States Educational Commission (Fulbright Program) enabled me to conduct year-long research in Kyoto. Supplemental and dissertation write-up funding was provided by the Social Science Research Council.

This book is dedicated to the anonymous performers, illustrators, authors, and copyists of long ago who created these stories and to the collectors and antiquarians who preserved them.

NOTES

1. *Gunsho ruijū* (Tokyo: Naigai shoseki kaisha, 1928), 25:503–504. I am grateful to Paul Varley for his advice in preparing this translation.

2. Many works of premodern Japanese literature are of uncertain authorship, but in most cases at least the social identity of its authors and audience is fairly clear. With otogi-zōshi, we have no such information. According to a once hotly debated theory, otogi-zōshi were produced by and for the class of self-governing townsmen that arose in the late Middle Ages. See Hayashiya Tatsusaburō, *Chūsei bunka no kichō* (Tokyo: Tokyo daigaku shuppankai, 1953). On the other hand, others have credited authorship to the culturally rich but economically faltering aristocracy attempting to inculcate their own values in the culturally impoverished townsmen who, they say, composed the major audience of otogi-zōshi. See, e.g., Sugiura Minpei, *Sengoku ran'yo no bungaku* (Tokyo: Iwanami shoten, 1965).

3. *Hikketsu no monogatari*, by Ishii Yasunaga, identified by a later copyist as a priest.

4. For a detailed study, see Barbara Ruch, "Medieval Jongleurs and the Making of a National Literature," in *Japan in the Muromachi Age*, ed. John W. Hall and Toyoda Takeshi (Berkeley: University of California Press, 1977).

5. Donald Keene, "Japanese Books and Their Illustrations," *Yearbook of Comparative and General Literature* 24 (1975): 6.

6. *Genji monogatari* has been translated into English as *The Tale of Genji* by both Arthur Waley (London: George Allen & Unwin, 1935) and Edward G. Seidensticker (New York: Knopf, 1976). Helen McCullough has translated the *Ise monogatari* as *Tales of Ise* (Stanford, Calif.: Stanford

University Press, 1968). Many of the better-known poems in the imperial anthologies have been translated in Robert Brower and Earl Miner's *Japanese Court Poetry* (Stanford, Calif.: Stanford University Press, 1961). For a highly engaging translation with commentary on the *Kokinshū,* see Laurel Rasplica Rodd and Mary Catherine Henkenius' *Kokinshū: A Collection of Poems Ancient and Modern* (Princeton, N.J.: Princeton University Press, 1984). "A Song of Unending Sorrow" can be found in *Anthology of Chinese Poetry,* ed. Cyril Birch (New York: Grove, 1965), pp. 266–269.

7. Particularly to *kana-zōshi,* which have also been prey to a similar characterization as mere precursors to the succeeding fictional genre of *ukiyo-zōshi.* In this way, Japanese literary genres are often stigmatized as transitional, their inherent qualities unremarked and unexplored.

8. Narrative forms similar to that of otogi-zōshi were anticipated in the late Heian period with the *Tsutsumi chūnagon monogatari* (compiled, interestingly enough, in the medieval period) and also appear in certain tales in late setsuwa collections.

9. *Muromachi jidai monogatari taisei,* ed. Yokoyama Shigeru and Matsumoto Ryūshin, 13 vols. (Tokyo: Kadokawa shoten, 1973–1987).

A Discretionary Tale

Otonashi sōshi

A Discretionary Tale takes the form of a sermon delivered by an omniscient narrator who freely comments on the actions and motivations of the fictional characters, condemning frivolity and commending discretion. All the stern admonitions of the narrator are not quite sufficient to tame the exuberance of his subject matter, however, and the story emerges less a didactic fable than a dry account of realpolitik of the bedroom, expressing a dominant ethic of opportunism and practical adaptation to circumstance. Everyone, even the hapless messenger, acts in what he perceives to be his own best interests, cheerfully manipulating and slandering others in order to further his own cause. In the end, even the narrator admits that the errant wife's sin of infidelity is minor in comparison to the graver sin of indiscretion.

The core story may have been inspired by an anecdote in the ninth book of the semihistorical chronicle *Masu kagami (The Greater Mirror)* in which a princess mistakes another man for her usual lover. When the lover arrives, he sees an oxcart already stationed outside her residence, and an attendant later reports that the princess has been entertaining another man.

This manuscript bears the date of 1570 and an imperial cipher. The copyist was probably Prince Seijin, the youngest son of Emperor Ōgimachi, who may have transcribed the story for writing practice. Prince Seijin died in 1586; in 1570 he would have been nineteen years old. The translation is based on the untitled, unannotated text printed in *Muromachi jidai monogatari taisei* (3:314–322), transcribed from a single illustrated scroll in the Akagi bunko collection. There are only two extant copies of this story; the other, also a single illustrated scroll, is in the collection of the Tokyo National Museum, which has kindly provided the illustrations reproduced here. Hagino Yoshiyuki, an early commentator on otogi-zōshi, created the title from a phrase appearing in the text when he discussed the story in his *Shinpen otogi-zōshi* (Tokyo: Seishidō shoten, 1901).

Not so long ago there occurred a silly and amusing affair. To start at the beginning of the tale, we must look to the capital near the river at Nishinotōin, where had long resided a husband and wife. This couple had been deeply in love from the moment they first set eyes on each other, and their boundless affection spanned the steepest of mountains and deepest of oceans. Never once throughout their many years together had the man left his wife alone.

There came a time, however, when, quite suddenly and unexpectedly, the husband found himself obliged to undertake a journey far away. He was sorely distressed at the prospect, for he was unaccustomed to travel and anticipated bitter loneliness. The woebegone face of the woman he was to leave behind told him that she shared his anguish. Together they lamented his long absence, wringing their tear-drenched sleeves. Never once did they dream that the waves of change would ever lap against their sturdy evergreen peaks of love. "My destination is to the west, so for me the capital will lie under the eastern skies. Let us each gaze at the moon as it rises over the mountains, and let it serve as a guide to our absent beloved," he said, trying his best to console her.

It was already well past the middle of the second month, and the third month was drawing closer. Still he lingered until the wild geese flew through the sky sparing not a glance at the blossoming trees of the capital. With such eagerness they flew to their homes in the north! He knew that he must depart at the break of day and was pained at the contrast between their anticipation and his burden of grief. Though it was difficult indeed to set out his traveling garb, he could not tarry long.

Tatsu yori mo
kokoro zukushi no
tabi koromo
tsuya keki sode o
itsu ka harawamu

After sadly setting out
in my traveling robes,
when may I brush the dew
from these glistening sleeves?[1]

And she returned:

Koto no ha no   Your words of parting
tsuyu okisoete   dew-drenched leaves,
ito mo nao   my sad self remaining
tomaru ukimi zo   ever more damp with tears.[2]
nure wa masareru

It was with infinite regret that his grieving wife watched his departure. In dreary solitude, she would gaze at the skies under which he
traveled, sorrowfully thinking of him.

Then a man who lived close by, whom she had frequently
encountered, secretly came to call on her.

"My desire for you is so overwhelming that I've wanted to speak
of it," he began. "Until now I have refrained for fear of appearances and passed the days aimlessly. Your reed fence is so close to
mine; we have wasted too much time behind our separate gates.
Now I can no longer keep my love hidden—will you be mine?
Never mind about gossip; social position is of no concern when one
is lost on the path of love!

"My own humble self hardly merits comparison with Prince

Genji, but it is said that an overwhelming passion led him to approach his stepmother Fujitsubo; the result of their secret liaison was the imperial prince named Reizei. Then again, a mistaken spring night's dalliance with the Lady of the Misty Moon led him to exile at Suma Bay, where his sad pallet and damp pillow of waves afforded him but brief moments of slumber in wakeful nights spent in a rustic cottage. Yet, out of an unbidden dream, he formed another bond, with the lady of Akashi.[3] Well, so too Middle Captain Narihira met with a bad turn of fate when his beloved was devoured by a demon.[4] He could no longer remain in the capital and went far off to the east in his traveling robes. At Utsu Mountain, thoughts of home crowded on him; at Suruga, he gazed at the smoke rising from Mount Fuji, and his heart was charred with memories. Yet soon he ended up in Musashino, following the endless pursuit of love. Am I of this era so very different from Narihira, the man of old? I shall surely die of unrequited love in this fleeting world of dreams! If you feel at all moved, please show me just a little sympathy!" he adroitly concluded.

The woman did not question his sincerity. Her heart was as fickle as a quickly fading flower dye. Indeed, it seems rare enough to find

fidelity lasting for a thousand or even a hundred days. She was as pliant as fragile bamboo grass to these trifling deceptions falling from the lips of a smooth talker—it took but an instant for her heart to be completely won over. Since the world itself is so unreliable, people's hearts also vary from one to another. There are those men who value a lifelong companion so much that they drown themselves in the sea if parted from their beloved; then there are those who weep and wail for a loved one, only to forget about him an instant later. Nothing lasts a lifetime with these people. It is a pity that such different hearts can occupy the same world! Ah, this world, where people cannot devote themselves faithfully to anything at all! This woman surrendered as easily as pampas grass bending to the first faint breeze wafting her way.

Each evening she would wait until frost rested on her haircords for her lover's flute to sound the signal of a chirping cricket. The

couple grew so foolhardy that he came calling every night without
fail, regardless of who might be watching. The woman's reserve
melted completely, and she became even more intimate with him
than with her husband of many years. Though they thought that
their affair was a well-kept secret, such is the way of the world that
gossip spreads easily, particularly since they had so repeatedly cast
their nets into forbidden waters. What folly it was to believe that
others would not catch on, when it was so very obvious to all! Soon
her eager anticipation and his secret visits became common knowledge, and the neighbors would gather together and whisper of
nothing else.

Among the gossipers was a young man who decided that he too
would make his own advances. Just as Prince Niou deceived Ukifune by wooing her in the guise of Kaoru,[5] so would he pretend to
be this woman's lover.

He bided his time until very late on a moonless night. Concealing himself in the shadows of a tree near her eaves, he blew a few notes on a flute and waited for the expected response.

Without the slightest idea of what was transpiring, the woman was eagerly anticipating her lover. About the time he was due to arrive, she heard the sound of a flute and assumed that the player could be none other than he. Without catching a clear look at his face, she tugged at his sleeve and led him inside, where she brought out sake and food.

"From past to present, people have always celebrated occasions like this," she told him. "There's a poem that speaks of downing over three hundred cups of wine.[6] When you are sad or lonely, you can drown your sorrows for a time in wine. It's a known fact that sake is an elixir of longevity and a tonic to the spirit, so you must never let your cup run dry." She entertained him with great familiarity. They drank together until both were quite giddy, then lay down.

It must have been well past midnight when her usual lover arrived. He sounded his flute and cleared his throat, but the house was locked up tight, and his mistress appeared to have gone to sleep. He wondered uneasily what might have gone wrong. He waited for a while until he heard the tolling of the late night bell, then, disappointed at the prospect of returning home alone, lost all sense of discretion and pounded at her door. There was no response from within. "She seems to have gone quite deaf!" he thought. "That's pretty suspicious! Just like the ever-changing Asuka River, her affections shift from day to day. This is not a lodging in the eastern provinces; why does she refuse me and raise the forbidding barrier of Nakoso?[7] How heartless she is!" And he recited as he bitterly returned home:

Tanomi naki	What was the point of her vow
hito no kokoro o	of everlasting love
hakanaku mo	when her fickle heart
nochi no yo kakete	is true but a moment?
nani chigirikemu	

Inside, the woman let forth a string of bitter complaints, never dreaming that the man lying beside her was anyone but her lover. "That man who was pounding at the door is so obnoxious! What must the neighbors think, with all that racket going on so late at night? Surely you've heard of him." And she pronounced his own name quite distinctly. "There are plenty of smart alecks around here, but he's by far the worst of them. He's so impertinent! He hides beneath trees under eaves, catcalling out to women passing by. He pulls all sorts of nasty pranks like that!" she said contemptuously.

Her companion heard her out and realized that she was speaking of none other than himself. With difficulty he managed to suppress his laughter. He had half a mind to announce his name and leave, but feared her wrath. "After all, if you're in a palace of logs . . ."⁸ he muttered to himself, and managed to conceal his identity by saying as little as possible. He returned home while it was still dark, delighted with himself for having managed the caper so well:

Omowazu wa	Unexpected though it was,
chigiri shi koto zo	I'll not forget those vows of love,
wasurarenu	though I know not
nochi no nasake wa	how long her affection may last.
shirazu nagara	

With no idea of her mistake, the woman was still vexed over the midnight pounding at her door. She called in a trustworthy man to bring her grievance to the culprit.

"It's not only that he gave me so much trouble, but he thinks nothing of disturbing the neighbors' sleep as well! They must be as upset as I am! Please go and complain to him," she said.

"I'll see what I can do about it," he replied, and left. Unaware that the person in question had been mistaken for another, the messenger assumed a severe expression and went to scold the man for his misconduct. Needless to say, the man to whom he addressed this grievance was the very one who had slept with her the night before.

"Her anger is justified, but, since it was the fellow she's so friendly with who raised the ruckus, you had better take her complaints over to him. *I* had nothing to do with it. I was strolling past her house last night, just minding my own business, when I saw her beckon. When I came closer to find out what she wanted, to my surprise she grabbed my sleeve and hauled me in. It was rather odd, but I didn't mind a bit! I'm not one to refuse an invitation like that! Clearly, she wanted me to spend the night with her. Well, she brought out loads of wonderful food and went on and on about the merits of drinking. She poured out sake, and I drank so much that I lost my senses. On her behalf, I was worried about appearances, so when I left I just kept my eyes fixed on the skies above. I never imagined that she'd send you to complain like this! If I had forced myself on her, then indeed I would be at fault, but, as it is, this is her own wrongdoing! When her husband off in the countryside returns, I'll tell him about this, even though I *am* involved!" he taunted.

The servant realized that the man had a case and was at a loss for

words. "I spoke without knowing the full circumstances. Please forgive me for having made such a fool of myself," he apologized, and left. He told his mistress just what he had heard, omitting not a single detail.

After she heard him out, she realized that she had only herself to blame. Her heart pounded, and she was in a state of shock. Now her concern over neighborhood gossip gave way to anguish and apprehension over her husband's reaction should he be told, and this misery was further compounded by the mortifying thought that word might leak out to her lover. She bitterly regretted her inability to change the past. "If only I somehow could take it all back!" she thought a hundred, a thousand times over. But once the seeds of evil begin to sprout, there is no way to take back words rashly uttered, no matter how hard one tries. There was nothing to be done about it: she had completely lost face.

"I've trusted you from the start. You mustn't allow the least dewdrop of this to spill out to anyone," she pleaded, sealing his lips with a great number of gifts. "Please try to appease his anger!"

Thus the poor man was entrusted with a mission as tenuous as a wisp of cloud. What in the world was he to say this time? The woman's evening trysts had been completely disrupted, and, though dawn may have brought regret over her unfortunate mistake, how was he to smooth it over as if nothing had ever happened? It would be hard indeed for his words to batter down the sharp rocks of the offended man's ire, but she had begged so much, and given him so many presents, that he found it impossible to refuse her. "I won't make the slightest error," he told her, and set out immediately.

The woman was in such a state that she could not distinguish dream from reality. In an excess of woe she recited:

> Kesa koso wa   If only this morn
> aranu hito to mo   I could turn it to a dream—
> shiratsuyu no   those dewy vows of love made
> musubu chigiri o   to one I knew not was another.
> yume ni nasabaya

Unable to refuse her pleas, the messenger had assured her that he would take care of everything, but now he wondered what he would say. The right words simply would not come. He was putting himself out for her at her request, yet, depending on how he managed it, he himself could end up as much a laughingstock as she. His good name would be lost in the waters of notorious Name-taking River. He recalled a fable of the emperor Gyō of China, who, on hearing of a loyal subject named Kyoyū living on Mount Ki, sent an imperial summons awarding him a court rank. Rather than send a reply, Kyoyū declared that his ears had been so polluted by such tidings that he was obliged to cleanse and purify them in the river. Sōfu, who lived on the same mountain, brought his ox to drink at the river. When he heard what had happened, he announced that he would never allow the beast to drink from such tainted water and led it home.[9]

"Loyal vassals of old valued purity of mind so much!" he thought. "How can I, brought into this nasty affair at her bidding,

possibly cleanse that besmirched soul, even if I bathe it in the
mightiest of oceans?" Just the thought of that old parable caused
him infinite shame. Still, he had to say something, so off he went
to call on the offended man.

"Well, now, I'm afraid that my lady spoke without any idea of
how rudely she was behaving. She regrets it deeply, and I have
come to offer her most sincere apologies. Fortunately, no one other
than you knows about this miserable mess. Please, I beg you to
keep it a secret."

Amused by this sudden shift from accusation to apology, the
other responded mockingly, "But she called me the most lecherous
pest around—she must hate me a great deal! What's more, I can't
imagine why she brought those baseless accusations against me. It's
extraordinarily spiteful of her!"

"You are absolutely correct. The fault lies solely with her, and
she begs your indulgence. Even enemies who have already sharp-
ened their swords for battle can make peace if they beg forgiveness.
She is truly frivolous and has but a woman's fickle sensibility. She
was carried away on a reckless course of action and is totally to
blame for having caused you so much trouble. It's a sorry mess, but
you did spend a sweet night with her and did experience an
uncommon love, so forgive her, won't you?" simpered the messenger obsequiously. He was gratified when the other broke into a
smile and replied in a mollified tone. "And if you were to lodge a
complaint against her," he continued, "it might be much harder
on you than just keeping quiet. Hateful though she is, if you cause
her such anguish as to make her die of shame, the burden of sin
would rest on you. It would be best to forget the whole thing." He
concluded by pouring out more apologies.

However annoying, it was all so terribly amusing that the man
decided to let the matter rest.

It was because the woman so openly and indiscreetly spoke out
that things came to such an unhappy state. What a pity that she
ended up looking so foolish! Had she just feigned innocence and
kept her affair a secret, this need never have happened. Truly, it is
painful even to hear of her horrible disgrace, far worse than death

itself. An admirable woman is one who, though perhaps not as outwardly beautiful as others, is noble at heart and maintains a modest, discreet demeanor in all things. She shows sensitivity and compassion regarding even couplings under cover of night.[10] Such a woman regards even careless words tossed out on the spur of the moment as forever binding and, though she may not be aware of their full implications, stands by them nonetheless.

A woman may be of high rank and lack any obvious flaws, but if her heart does not match her looks—if she lies, offends others, and behaves immodestly—then the blossoms of her beauty will wither to the beholder. Her appearance will reflect the state of her heart, and her external charms will fade. Such a woman has no deep appreciation of poetry; she is worthless and despicable. How sad!

Be she of high or low standing, if she does just as she pleases without regard for the opinions of others, sooner or later she is bound to cause a scene and become an object of gossip.

Of course, there is no such thing as an unblemished woman, perfect in all respects. Still, it is sufficient that she be eternally vigilant about her reputation and gentle at all times. Those who do just as they please inevitably invite the censure of others. Whether noble or base, a woman should comport herself in a manner befitting her position and always take care to behave properly.

Thirteenth year of Eiroku (1570)
Early summer, middle of the month
The last child of the Emperor, aged nineteen[11]

NOTES

1. The poem puns on *tatsu*, "to depart" and "to cut out" (clothing).

2. This poem employs associative terms *(engo)* of the preceeding "dew" and "sleeves," *ha*, "leaves," and *tomaru*, "to remain." The conceits in these two poems are common in poems of parting and travel.

3. The suitor is attempting to turn the woman's head with references to well-known episodes of secret passion in *The Tale of Genji*, although this litany of passions gone awry will strike the reader as a rather ineffective form of wooing. The reference to the Lady of Akashi might be an intimation that, like Prince Genji in exile, the husband's attentions may have turned elsewhere.

4. The remainder of the suitor's monologue refers to *The Tales of Ise*. He uses these classical allusions to display his erudition and convince the woman that forming new attachments on the heels of the old had precedents in the classical literary corpus.

5. Another allusion to *The Tale of Genji*.

6. This allusion is unclear.

7. A complicated wordplay involving *nakoso*, the name of a barrier gate homophonous with "do not come." Also seen in *The Errand Woman*.

8. An allusion to a conceit appearing in several poems, linking the log palace of the old capital with a lover's anonymity.

9. This Chinese parable of the legendary Emperor Yao and his loyal subject Hsü Yu is often cited in medieval Japanese literature as an example of purity of mind.

10. A general approximation of an elaborate but common wordplay on *yo no ukifushi:* the sad things of this world/nighttime sexual activity. There is a tertiary pun involving bamboo (*yo*, "stalk"; *fushi*, "joint"), also seen in *Lazy Tarō*.

11. The colophon is followed by an imperial cipher *(kaō)*.

The Cat's Tale

Neko no sōshi

The Cat's Tale is based on an actual edict ordering the release of all cats in the city of Kyoto, recorded by Nishi no Saiin Tokiyoshi in his diary entry on the fourth day of the tenth month, 1602: "It is not permitted to restrain cats; they have been set free for three months now." Although Tokiyoshi does not describe the circumstances that led to such an edict, it may have been prompted less by humanitarian impulses than by a burgeoning rat population. If this story is any indication of the outcome, the emancipation of cats must have quickly brought the rat infestation under control.

The Cat's Tale takes the form of a hearing in which two species put their respective cases before a holy man, who tries without success to persuade each to mend its evil ways. As is common with fictional accounts of animals, the behavior of the cats and rats is rendered in human terms and their faults and foibles rationalized through comparison to analogous human failings.[1] The world of *The Cat's Tale* is one of brutality and upheaval, in which Buddhist dogma of nonviolence is seldom heeded in the daily struggle for survival. Having been lashed by years of political and military strife, late medieval Japan had seen bitter proof of the law that a flourishing species is ready prey to another on the ascendency. As expressed in one of the concluding poems, a dog follows on the heels of every cat who has caught a mouse.

This translation is based on the annotated text in *Otogi-zōshi,* ed. Ichiko Teiji, Nihon koten bungaku taikei 38 (Tokyo: Iwanami shoten, 1958), pp. 297–306, from the Shibukawa Seiemon illustrated printed booklet set of the *Otogi-bunko* in the Ueno Library, Tokyo. The illustrations are from a similar edition and are provided through the courtesy of the Tokyo University Library. It should be noted that the Japanese term *nezumi* refers to both rats and mice, which in English conjure up completely different images. For the sake of internal coherence, I have rendered it as *mouse,* although the cats in the tale would certainly cast their votes in favor of *rat.*

All beings, men and beasts alike, know that the peace and security of the realm are due to excellent governance. Truly, these blessed times surpass even the fabled illustrious reigns of the emperors Go and Shun.[2]

In the middle of the eighth month of the year 1602, an edict was issued freeing all the cats in the capital. To this end, there was posted on the corner of First Avenue a notice from the city magistrate. It proclaimed:

> All cat's fetters are to be loosened; cats shall be released and allowed to roam at will. Furthermore, all trade in cats must cease. Those who disregard this decree shall be severely punished. Thus it is ordered.

As a result of this ordinance, each and every cat who formerly had been carefully guarded was tagged[3] and released. The overjoyed cats ran and leaped all over town celebrating their new-found freedom. They found this holiday to be exhilarating and a wonderful opportunity to catch mice.

It was not long before the terrified mice ran for cover. No longer did they scurry about in the corridors or rafters, and, when they did venture abroad, they were forced to creep along silently without

making the slightest squeak. All the townsmen hoped that the edict would continue to be vigilantly enforced.

To the north of the city lived a most venerable recluse who had shed all evil and followed only the righteous. In the morning he would pray that the heavens and earth would endure forever, in the evening that the world be at peace, that he be felicitously reborn in heaven, and that the entire universe eventually would receive the benefit of Buddhist teachings. He possessed a clear understanding of the dual teachings of doctrine and meditation, and his great virtue moved clergy and laity, men and women alike, to tears of admiration. Truly, he might well have been called a Great Universal Buddha.[4]

It would seem that even the birds and beasts knew of this holy man's remarkable devotion, for one night he had a strange dream in which a mouse priest appeared to him.

"I am taking great liberties in addressing Your Reverence, but day and night, from dawn to dusk, I continually listen to your sermons from underneath the veranda. When I heard you say that one may lessen sins through confession, I decided to venture forth. If I sincerely regret and confess my sins, would you be so gracious as to favor me with a few words of wisdom?" he begged.

The priest was astonished that such a creature could speak with such refinement. "It is said that everything in existence, even nonsentient plants and trees, can achieve Buddhahood," he responded. "How much more, then, can you mice, who are living beings, erase countless sins in an instant if you but place your trust in the Savior Buddha! According to the teaching, both the Savior and the Pure Land exist nowhere but in your own hearts, within easy reach. Even birds and beasts cannot fail to become buddhas through this doctrine."

"Well, then, allow me to tell my tale of confession," said the mouse, brushing away his tears. "Because all the cats in the capital have been released, every single one of us mice has either hidden in the shadows, run away, or perished. Those few who still remain are hanging on by a thread. We cower in misery behind foundation stones and under verandas, never relaxing our guard even a whis-

ker's breadth. We try to make our homes in burrows, but within a
day or two they become so stuffy that we cannot bear to stay. When
we venture out into the world, those blasted cats pounce on us, bit-
ing ferociously, slashing and ripping our flesh. Our karma from a
previous life must be bad indeed to have produced such misery as
this!"

Responded the priest, "The conditions you lament are certainly
pitiful. Now that I've imparted the teaching to you, you are as a
disciple to me, and I am compelled to tell you why you are the
objects of all this hatred. I myself, a lone priest, repaper an
umbrella and set it aside to dry, soon to find the handle gnawed to
bits in no time at all. When I prepare roasted beans and snacks to
entertain the deacons, the food disappears overnight. You manage
to chew holes not only in my robes and clerical garb but in my fans,
books, screens, rice cakes, and bean curd! No matter how forbear-
ing a priest I may be, it's only natural that I'd want to kill you! You
can't expect ordinary people to react any differently!"

"I share your opinion," responded the mouse. "And I try to tell
the younger mice to change their ways, but, as they say, good
advice is painful to the ears and good medicine bitter to the
tongue. They pay me no heed whatsoever, but just go on urging
each other to more and more mischief. I've told them not to incur
people's ire: to stop pillaging houses everywhere, stealing servants'

aprons, people's socks, robes, and skirt edging, stashing them in the corners of trunks, bundles, and baskets to make their nests. I've told them to stop gnawing on things that neither nourish nor benefit them and to refrain from creeping around the edges of pots. I've told them since they were red-skinned infants and young mouslings, but they do just as they please, making their nests in people's pillows, mats, ceilings, and old roofs. They do nothing but these awful things . . . such hopeless creatures!"

Just then the priest awoke to find that day had already broken.

The next night he had another dream in which a yellow tiger-striped cat appeared and spoke earnestly to him.

"I have received word that Your Reverence's great virtue has inspired a certain rodent, scurrilous of heart and despised by humans though he is, with the audacity to come here and address you. That rat of a mouse speaks the very height of blasphemy! No sooner do you bless him with compassion than he's sure to filch something from you! Allow me to give you a rough idea of our feline pedigree. Please listen to me! In coming to speak with you, I run the risk of seeming to compete with those mice, but, without knowing our circumstances, you might think badly of us." He arched his back, and his sharp eyes glittered.

"We are descendants of the tiger, who inspires such awe in India and Cathay. Japan is a small country, so we adjusted our size accordingly when we crossed over. This is the reason why there are no tigers in Japan. In the reign of Emperor Engi, we were high in imperial favor; one of us was loved by Kashiwagi and kept close to his side.[5] Then, in the reign of Emperor Go-Shirakawa, we were restrained by leashes and kept close to his side. Yet, thus tethered, if a mouse runs around even an inch away from our noses, we can catch it only in spirit. When we are thirsty, we purr and cry for water, only to be slapped into silence. The pain is terrible! People think that we can't speak, but we communicate in the sacred Sanskrit of India, which is unintelligible to the men of this country. Our lot in life has been one of leashes and lashes. But the all-encompassing mercy of the gods has extended to the likes of cats, just as the moon bestows its light on even a wretched shack. We are

profoundly grateful that they have released our bonds and lessened our suffering. Each morning we face the rising sun, fervently pur-raying for this reign of the sovereign to last ever long."

Said the priest in response, "You speak profoundly indeed. This brings to mind the parable about Nanzen killing a cat: though it may be severed in two, how can a cat possibly be other than a cat?⁶ Even so, this raises a problem: as a holy man, I am duty bound to intervene when I witness a situation like this. According to the law of karmic cycles, a killer of flesh is doomed to die, only to be reborn, then to die once again, bound to the endless, inescapable wheel of karma. Only by realizing the emptiness of all things may you release yourselves from the myriad evils of birth and death, cease to wander the Three Worlds and Six Realms,⁷ and achieve immediate release. Stop your killing! Why don't you try to make your meals of cuttlefish and rice or an occasional dried sardine, her-ring, or salmon?"

"You're absolutely right, but stop a minute and think: a diet of rice nourishes humans, stoking their innards and allowing their limbs to move vigorously and their mouths to speak adroitly; the flavor of rice is enhanced by the addition of delicacies from the seas and mountains. In the same way, a diet of mice, provided through the benevolence of the gods above, enables us to leap and fly about in robust health as well as any bird. What's more, we are able to take leisurely afternoon naps in the expectation of later dining on mice. You must understand that no cat would agree to renounce that!"

This endlessly compassionate priest was unable to respond, but sat shedding mute tears, his very soul shattered. Thus the dream ended.

Toward dawn he had another dream, this time of the mouse, who declared, "At this rate we can no longer remain in the capital." Then mice from throughout the city gathered together and sent out a message to their comrades: the group from Nishijin was to go to the foot of Funaoka Mountain, the group from Kogawa to the woods by Goryō Shrine, the group from Tachiuri to the woods by Shōkoku Temple, the group from Juraku to the Kitano Woods, and the group from downtown to Rokkaku Temple.

All the mice in their respective meeting places discussed their predicament. The wisest of them came forward, saying, "After all, given this catastrophe, it looks as if we won't have any choice but to take our own lives. How in the world can we save our skins now?" They all conferred together.

"It has already been fifty days since the cats were freed," he continued. "And since then not even a fishbone has passed our lips, nor have we caught a whiff of fried bean curd or chicken! Even if we do manage to avoid the cats, we'll surely die of starvation.

"However, I seem to have heard that the farmers in Ōmi[8] haven't harvested their rice because of a tax census—yes, I do think that's so. Let us remove ourselves there for the winter. We can have the women and children hole up under the rice plants and make it through the winter. When the year ends and the weather turns warm again, with the help of the god Jizō we will flee to hideouts in nearby mountains, fields, temples, and towns.[9] If we can find a boat, we'll cross over to the islands in Lake Biwa. We can dig up mountain potatoes and bracken for food, and perhaps we'll be able to prolong our lives for a time.

"More than anything else, I shall miss the coming New Year's

delicacies—the round rice cakes, the petal-shaped cakes, the crackers and candies. And I had so counted on passing the idle hours of spring rain nibbling and squeaking around! What a pity that we have to leave on account of those despicable cats! But the cats are also being chased hither and yon by *their* enemies, the dogs. I see them fallen by the wayside or at the river's edge, soaked with rain and mud, and get great satisfaction from knowing that they've received their just desserts."

With that thought, the mice took heart and scampered off here and there. Those refined mice who had long resided in aristocratic homes composed some clumsy verses in parting:

Nezumi toru	Behind the cat
neko no ushiro ni	catching a mouse
inu no ite	stands a dog:
nerau mono koso	the hunter becomes the hunted.
nerawarenikeri	
Arazaran	I may not be around for long,
kono yo no naka no	but I'd like to take with me
omoide ni	a memory of a world
ima hito tabi wa	catless for once.[10]
neko naku mogana	

Ji ji to ieba	Whenever we squeak,
kikimimi tatsuru	listening ears perk up;
nekodono no	how frightful it is,
manako no uchi no	the piercing gleam of a cat's eye!
hikari osoroshi	

The priest was afraid that if he told others what he had witnessed, they might spread rumors that he had lost his mind, so he decided to keep it to himself. But these strange dreams were so fascinating that he could not resist relating them to a close friend, who found them very amusing. Nonetheless, just as the monk had said, mice grew fewer in numbers and no longer stole or frolicked at bedsides.

From the past to the present, one is grateful for this degree of public order. With a splendid sovereign and a prosperous people, this felicity shall continue everlong, and the heart knows naught but gladness!

NOTES

1. *The Cat's Tale* is somewhat similar to *The Tale of the Mouse*, translated by D. E. Mills in *Monumenta Nipponica*, 34:2 (1979). Both feature priests confronted by mice who cleverly defend their destructive activities and recite amusing poetry. Mills notes that this manuscript is very different from two other otogi-zōshi tale versions of the same title, which feature marriages between mice and humans.

2. The Chinese emperors Yao and Shun, often upheld as examples of superior rulers.

3. Presumably with the owner's name?

4. *Dainichi nyōrai*, the central buddha in the Shingon pantheon.

5. A reference to an episode in *The Tale of Genji*. Owing to a fracas caused by a princess' cat, Kashiwagi falls in love with the princess and manages to procure the cat, of which he is exceedingly fond.

6. A well-known Zen *koan* about monks who were fighting over a kitten; the head priest Nanzen killed it when none could utter a word to save its life.

7. *Sangai rokushū rinne*, transmigration through the three worlds (the

realms of desire, form, and nonform) and the six paths (hell, hungry ghosts, animals, warriors, men, and heavenly beings).

8. To the north of the capital.

9. Here appears a long list of place names in and around the Ōmi area, deleted in the interest of narrative continuity.

10. A humorous transformation of a poem attributed to the poetess Izumi Shikibu, in the *Go shūishū:* "Arazaramu / kono yo no naka no / omoide ni / ima hitotabi no / au koto mogana" (I shall soon be no more, / yet to meet just once / would give me a memory / to take to the beyond).

Old Lady Tokiwa
Tokiwa no uba

The medieval Japanese sensibility, so heavily steeped in Buddhist doctrine, frequently gave narrative expression to the conflict between physical desires and spiritual aspirations. Most explorations of this theme concern tonsured male hermits and their battles against the temptations of the flesh; *Old Lady Tokiwa* presents a highly unusual portrait of a woman remaining within the world while trying to cast off all attachments. Not surprisingly, she finds that, however willing the spirit, the flesh is weak. Gradually she begins to punctuate her prayers with supplications for nourishment and attention, vividly evoking the tension between mundane and spiritual drives. The result is a bittersweet depiction of the mental and physical plight of the aged and the callous indifference of loved ones.

It is obvious from her many appeals to the mercy of the Amida Buddha that the old woman is a believer in the widely popular Pure Land Buddhism, which holds that rebirth in the blissful Pure Land may be assured through sincere invocation of the name of the Savior Buddha. Despite her many digressions and lapses, at the end of the tale she is clearly shown to achieve salvation. This kind of proverbial "happy ending," so common to medieval Japanese tales, seems rather unjustified and artificial given the extremely dismal picture that has been painted throughout. It does, however, prove the efficacy of sincere, if muddled, prayer and thus situates the tale in conformity with both the requirements of the genre and Amidist teachings. The reader will see that her digressions become more elevated in subject as they move from bodily concerns with food and drink to love and poetry, perhaps reflecting the old lady's spiritual progress.

Unlike most other didactic tales of spiritual salvation, *Old Lady Tokiwa* lacks the strong narratorial voice that normally alerts the reader to the lessons embedded in the tale. For the most part, the text consists of minimally narrated, untagged soliloquoy with no clear distinction drawn between interior thought and spoken monologue, a highly effective device that reinforces the image of a confused, rambling old woman. This run-together quality makes the task of determining speaker extremely difficult. I have chosen to treat the bulk of the text as an unmediated transcription of the old woman's monologue, but it should be noted that in several places lines spoken by the old woman could be rendered equally as either internal thought or narrator-delivered lines. The illustration captions have been incorporated into the main narrative, with each such incorporation clearly marked in the notes.

This translation is based on the unannotated text printed in *Muromachi jidai monogatari taisei* (10:125–133). The manuscript, housed in the Keio Library, is untitled. It is the oldest of five copies and one of the oldest extant Nara ehon, tentatively dated no later than the Keichō era, 1596–1615. At the time this book went to press, the manuscript was undergoing restoration, and its illustrations were unavailable for photographic reproduction.

In the land of Yamato there once lived a person called Old Lady Tokiwa.[1] Once she had been blessed with prosperity and happiness, but, as the years passed, her husband died, and her many children no longer paid her any attention or respect. She grew old and thought to herself, "Times of long ago have now passed, and bleak indeed is the prospect of old age. Through the dawns and dusks and the daily openings and closings of my brushwood door, I have been heedless to my many accumulated sins. This life has been in vain; what shall I do about the life to come?

"In the morning of youth, one takes pride in oneself, never realizing that, by the twilight years, that self becomes a mere pile of bleached bones. The twisted mass of human innards resembles only a huge coiled serpent. When adorning the face with cosmetics and clinging to carnal love, one is merely seeing value in a stinking corpse. The white bones of a body lying in a field fall asunder the instant they rot away from the flesh that once bound them together. In hell, sins take the form of blades slicing through the flesh, a forest of swords slashing at corpses.[2] How miserable to be frozen in the ice of Red Lotus Hell[3] or to drink scorching infernal flames![4]

"I observe the abode of this ephemeral flesh, and I see that it lacks even the precarious perch of a rootless weed at the edge of a precipice and that existence itself is but a mere boat adrift in a bay. I perceive the transient nature of this world and see that even the young and healthy would do well to reject it. As for me, my own body is aged, my head frosted, and my brows drooping. My face bears the waves of the four seas; my eyes are clouded over, my ears deaf, my mouth dry, my breathing labored, my teeth fallen out, and my back as bent as a bow. My figure mortifies even me; my skin is rough and my weakened knees about to give way any moment. I have prolonged my useless life in vain and am embarrassed at being seen by my children. If only I could say my prayers and die!"

The old lady suddenly awoke to the truth of Amida's vow to save all sentient beings who desired salvation. "Just watch me, Amida!"

she announced. As soon as she had washed and gargled to purify herself, she faced west and bowed low. "Oh Amida Buddha of the West! Please send me to the Western Paradise and grant me good karma!"

As the night wore on, she continued to pray. "How miserable I am! I'd like a little water, Amida. Warm or cold, either will do, but just give me some. And, while you're at it, will you take me to paradise right away? Oh, Amida Buddha! Aren't you there? Or aren't you listening? Isn't my voice reaching you? I'm praying for my very own salvation, not for others, and if I hear that you've ignored me and sent others to paradise, I'll be angry with you for a long, long time! Make sure that doesn't happen!"

Her children heard her prayers and, rather than sympathize with her plight, were both amused and contemptuous. "Listen to her at her devotions!" they said. "She thinks that heaven won't let her in unless she shouts. What a din she's raising! That typical shrill whine of the aged has been going on night after night." No one encouraged her; all ordered her to stop. What a pity!

"I've grown old raising all of you," the old lady told them. "What you've relied on in the past changes as swiftly as the rapids and shoals of the Asuka River, and you never know what tomorrow may bring. It's a shame that you don't show me any compassion. If I had asked you to spend morning and night at my side, I would indeed be hateful, but you haven't even come to see me once in ten days. It's even sadder when I hear of the piety of Hakuyū,[5] who grieved at the weakness of the blows given him by his mother, or of Teiran,[6] who used a wooden figure to remind him of his dear departed mother. If only you knew the truth of the teachings of filial piety! There may be the example of the evil king who harmed his father,[7] but how can you ridicule the mother who nursed and cherished you? Indeed, I think badly of you all, but here I am thinking of my offspring again when I should be calling on the Amida Buddha."

But, as is usual with the elderly, there was no end to her requests. "Hail Amida Buddha! I'd like some sake! How my back hurts! My knees hurt! My throat is parched! My children are near, but they don't even call to me. I'm so sad and lonely! Hail Amida Buddha!"[8] Her children gathered nearby and cocked their ears to hear her.

"Isn't there anything to eat? I'm starving! Are there any nice persimmons? If only I could eat some toasted rice cakes covered with bean jelly or drink some warm white rice gruel! If only I could have some citron, oranges, mandarin oranges, pomegranates, chestnuts, persimmons, jujubes, plums, apples, or pears![9] If only I could eat some loquats, wild peaches, strawberries, cranberries, or hackberries! How wretched I am!

"I'd like some green laver or some seaweed. I haven't a single tooth left in my mouth, but I could manage with my gums, except that the kelp might give me problems. I want some green laver, sweet laver, plumed laver, and all kinds of other seaweed as well. Hail Amida Buddha! How painful this is!

"And things from the mountains—if only I could have some yams, bracken sprouts, arrowroot, pine mushrooms, agaric, yellow lichens, grains, brown mushrooms, smooth mushrooms, sorrel mushrooms, broom mushrooms, purple mushrooms, or button mushrooms!

"Well, then, there's just no way to describe the fish I'd like— carp, young sweet smelt, sea trout, chub, bream, or sea bass . . . as much as I can eat! If only I could have some boar, chicken, rabbit, raccoon, or badger—I'd eat it stewed. How I'd like some abalone, turban shells, river shells, or clams!

"I'm so ashamed to ramble on about food! Not for a moment can I stop thinking about how to get my hands on a jam dumpling! Hail Amida Buddha! I want to say my prayers, but if you don't give me something to eat, I might not be able to go on![10]

"I'd like some of that tea I drank when I was young. I still can't forget the aroma of tea! I wish I could eat some sweet cakes, hot noodles, jam buns, iced noodles, warm gruel, bean jelly, fried food, dried food, or boiled food! If only I could forget about all the food I used to eat! Hail Amida Buddha!

"I have many children—if only they would come to visit. To what end did I raise them, they who now bring me only grief?

When they were little, they wanted for nothing, and I fed them without their even asking. Now, when I want something so much, they give me only hatred. I thought only of their needs: throughout the hottest days of summer I fanned them in their beds; on bitter winter nights I slept on the bare floor and covered them with thick quilts to protect them from cold drafts. They've completely forgotten their debt, thrust me aside, and shut me away where no one else lives. Even my great grandchildren despise me! How I wish to go to the Pure Land quickly!

"Insects of summer, which gather to the flame, deer of autumn, drawn to the sound of a flute, and all other warm-blooded beasts, including birds, are foolishly attached to their offspring. I've considered hurling myself into the pools or rapids of a river to drown. Even the endlessly compassionate Buddha died at the age of eighty-one, and here I am brazenly living on past ninety. I, who esteem the wisdom of Monjū and his doctrine of limitless compassion, who cherish the teaching of Fugen and his doctrine of limitless truth—no wonder my children hate me!"

So she thought, but continued nonetheless, "I want some sake, some stewed carp!" Thoughout the long autumn nights and long spring days, she never once forgot her craving for food. She dozed off and saw food in her dreams; she awoke, and food seemed to dance before her eyes. Each night she would wait for someone to bring her something to eat, until, chilled to the bone by storms and bitter winds, her strength gave out and she collapsed.

"I may not be a dappled pony, but if I were, the more I ate, the more my limbs would grow strong, and I could travel a hundred, even a thousand miles in a single day. I regret having had them at all, but I do have children, nay, even grandchildren—would not I venture into such dangerous places as a field where a tiger lies on their behalf?[11]

"If I had my molars and incisors, I could eat green plums and dried chestnuts. Why, I'd sing a song if someone asked me to! The lamp is dim, but I can hear just fine in the dark, and if I weren't worried about what people might say, I'd even walk around on stilts!"

Out of sheer loneliness, she arose and went out to the street corner for amusement, but the little urchins outside all laughed at her. "What a pitiful state I'm in! Hail, Amida Buddha! How painful! My stomach is empty! My back hurts!"

"Is she talking about herself? . . . What a pity, the state she's in. . . . What a shame!" came various comments from people passing by. "Please don't trip, granny! . . . How frightening! I can't get away from her! . . . She must be crazy! . . . Try to guess whether that's a monkey or an old lady. . . . How do you feel? . . . How miserable—she's so thin. She certainly is lonely." "Yes, she's absolutely miserable," commented a young girl. "What a racket she's raising, all by herself," added a young matron.[12]

The old woman was roused to fury, reminding them all of a demented character in a *sarugaku* or *dengaku* performance. She went back and looked at her reflection in a washbasin; to her shock, she saw only a dried-up demon.

"I'm not a beggar . . . there's no point in wearing these ragged hempen robes!" she cried, returning to her post by the brushwood door. Tears streamed down her face, but no one responded with a kind word.

"I cannot return to the past and relive it over and over again as the turns of a spool, so it is useless to remember it," she thought. "In the past, General Genji, compelled to secrecy, visited Fujitsubo and made his vows of love. And Kashiwagi fell in love with someone he'd barely glimpsed when her blind was raised. The lovely deep colors of the flowering branch beyond his grasp attracted him, and, in his foolish yearning, he recited, 'I leave . . . from whence the dew.' And she responded, '. . . could I but disappear into the sky.' He loved her so much that it seemed he left his soul on her sleeve when he departed. Ah, the jumbled robes of that dawn! I too have had a love like that!"[13]

As she chanted her prayers, her heart was filled with thoughts of Ariwara no Narihira.[14] "Languishing after a secret love, he lodged among the dew in the grasses at Musashino. Of the many hands that pulled at him were those of the Ise Virgin, who pledged her love under the moonlight, in a brief tryst broken at dawn. Her poem 'Did you come, or did I go . . .' and his response 'I was lost in the pitch-black darkness of the heart . . .' attested to the feelings they shared.[15] Please, Amida, look on this old woman with compassion!

"Kaoru parted the dense grasses and made of Ukifune a substitute for the dead Oigimi.[16] Then, unbeknownst to Kaoru, Niou also exchanged vows with her. When Niou departed at dawn, she knew that she must die. Deeply in love, the two crossed the river to the small isle of oranges and there spent a peaceful spring day, never tiring of gazing at each other. In the end, she determined to become one with the flotsam floating in the waves of the Uji River. My sadness is just as great as that of poor Ukifune, who nightly drowned in a flood of her own tears.

"Oh, I want some sake! My throat is parched! Come autumn, the wild geese that once parted through spring haze never fail to return to their homes; blossoms scattered by gales always bloom anew in spring. They come but for a moment, serving as examples of the transience of all things. It's no use regretting their passing. My once black hair is now white, and nothing is more painful than seeing my face in the mirror aged overnight. The past now seems but a dream, and I pass sleepless nights, my tears falling ceaselessly.

"When I was young, my beauty was as the maidenflower fluttering in a storm, the wild pink bending to the dew, the green willow rustling in the sudden stir of a nightingale's wings, the white chrysanthemum pure as a silk cocoon, or the ever-changing primrose in full bloom, dripping with evening dew. I remember times when my beauty was likened to an orange blossom. Once all eyes rested on me, but now my children hate me, and nary a soul likens me to a flower. I, who was once as lovely as a blossom of spring, who radiated the glow of the moon, am despised by my own flesh and blood. I am just like golden brocade in the dark, unnoticed and unremarked. When I was young, I loved and was loved in turn. The likes of Narihira, Sanekane, and Prince Genji[17] all longed for me. I cannot forget the past, when, in service at the Palace of Long Life, the august Emperor came to me late at night and we exchanged vows to be two birds sharing one wing in the world to come.[18] I may not be at the court of the bright sun, but the rain beating against the window fills me with sadness.

"I am not unlike the withered old Ono no Komachi:[19] once I was loved by all men, aristocrat and commoner alike, treasured on diases in exquisite pavilions, and adored by lofty nobility. Now it is all but a dream. I even performed the dance 'Rainbow Skirt and Heavenly Robe' under the spring blossoms of Mount Tainan and the autumn moon at the imperial palace.[20] I used to wear exquisite footwear—slippers or clogs—but now my children provide only rough open sandals for my feet. I wore precious silks, Korean damasks, and figured brocades and reclined on woolen rugs, but now, despised by my children, I lie on a tattered straw mat. Ah, how squalid! My poor body! If they would just give me a few fox or weasel skins I could rest my back on them. There is no misty moon of spring, nor do I have anything to lie on.[21] Shall I use my robes as a cushion and sleep in a weed-choked lodging?[22] I am not Komachi, but perhaps I shall perish in a field.[23] Ah me! What am I to do in this world of painful endurance? Please carry me away, Kannon and Seishi, ye two disciples of Amida!"

And she mounted the platform,[24] all the while saying her prayers. Invoking the name of Amida, she lay prostrate facing west and presently breathed her last. Flowers rained down, and the air was filled with a rare fragrance. There can be no doubt that she achieved salvation in her future life.

This has been the record of Old Lady Tokiwa, who came to a felicitous end. How marvelous! Hail Amida Buddha!

NOTES

1. *Tokiwa* means "everlasting" or "evergreen" and was also used as a personal name. Here, it probably serves as a nickname to poke fun at her longevity.
2. This describes the torments of the first of the eight great Buddhist hells.

3. The Red Lotus Hell is so called because the cold freezes the flesh to resemble a red lotus.

4. A reference to the searing heat of the sixth and seventh levels of the eight great Buddhist hells.

5. The Chinese admonitory tale of Bai Yü was well known to contemporary Japanese. When the son was late in bringing his mother's meals, he dutifully submitted to beatings.

6. The story of Ting Lan, an exemplary Chinese figure of filial piety, is recounted in *The Tale of the Brazier*.

7. Reference unclear.

8. The old lady's spoken lines, beginning with "Hail Amida Buddha! . . ." constitute part of the caption to illustrations 1 and 2. The remainder of the caption is too garbled for translation, but it seems to read: "What a trial! Sir, attend to your mother. / Children, go to your mother. / Oh, how awful (young master and bride) / You must come here. / Behave yourself. How nice! (nurse) [?]." Words that identify speakers of the lines are enclosed in parentheses.

9. Many of the varieties of food mentioned in the following catalogs are native to Japan and difficult to translate. The English-language approximations may not correspond to actual English terms. The difficulty is exacerbated by the many synonyms and redundancies, most probably included for rhythmic and repetitious effect. Where two terms are essentially redundant, I have collapsed them into one.

10. This line is somewhat unclear, particularly the ending: "kū no moshi [moji?] ga tabeseneba, setsu no hō domo iinubeshi." The translation represents more guesswork than anything else.

11. These lines are somewhat cryptic. Alternatively, she may be saying the opposite, that her ties to her children and her age prevent her from risking danger.

12. The comments of the passersby constitute the captions to illustrations 3 and 4, recast into the narrative.

13. This paragraph refers to episodes in *The Tale of Genji*. The two partially cited lines of poetry are from the second "Wakana" chapter.

14. A poet famed as a great lover, featured in *The Tales of Ise*.

15. From episode 69 of *The Tales of Ise*.

16. This paragraph resumes the reference to *The Tale of Genji*.

17. Paradigmatic romantic lovers.

18. A reference to the famous Chinese poem "The Song of Unending Sorrow."

19. A poet known for her beauty and passionate verse, said to have ended her life as a wrinkled crone.

20. Another allusion to "The Song of Unending Sorrow."

21. Through an elaborate poetic device, the misty moon of spring is often linked to bedding *(shiku mono)*. The import of the line is unclear.

22. An allusion to a poem in episode 3 of *The Tales of Ise:* "Omoi araba / mugura no yado ni / ne mo shinan / hijikimono ni wa / sode o shitsutsu" (If you love me / let us sleep together / lying on our spread sleeves / in a weed-choked hovel).

23. According to legend, Komachi died in a field.

24. *Kōza,* a raised seat for lecturers or preachers. This seems to indicate that the action of the story takes place at a temple, but the proximity of her children would indicate otherwise.

The Mirror Man
Kagami otoko emaki

The Mirror Man is an interesting primitive example of narrative splicing in otogi-zōshi. It may have been produced when two separate tales were recited or read sequentially, then later linked together by storytellers or scribes. The first half of the story belongs to the *Matsuyama kagami* folktale tradition telling of a marital spat sparked by a man's introduction of a mirror into his household, with versions appearing in the *Shintōshū* tale collection and the *kyōgen* play *Kagami otoko;* the latter half is redolent of legends of hidden villages and underworld kingdoms suffused with magic, recounted in folktales and several other otogi-zōshi.

While awkwardly plotted and often inconsistent, *The Mirror Man* derives a certain internal coherence from the mirror itself. In Japan, the mirror has long been considered a sacred object imbued with the spirit of the gods and powers to ward off evil. It was a precious object available only to the wealthy until the latter part of the medieval period, when the production of copper mirrors put them into the hands of those of more limited means. This story appeared in the period when the image of the mirror was shifting from the sacred to the mundane; thus, while the mirror is depicted in a humorous light, it still retains the otherworldly mystique that would lead the credulous man to regard it as demonic. The utopia he later discovers is populated by immortal women, familiars of the goddess Benten, and mice, traditionally associated in Japan with wealth and prosperity. Indeed, it might be that this is the world the man initially supposed to exist within the mirror. *The Mirror Man* demonstrates the mirror's ability to reward those who recognize its magical properties, and the story itself can be seen as a metaphor of fertility and prosperity.

This translation is based on the text transcribed from an illustrated scroll in the National Diet Library Collection, printed without annotations in *Muromachi jidai monogatari taisei* (3:387–389); the illustrations are from the same scroll and are provided through the courtesy of the National Diet Library.

Long ago in a village on a mountainside in the province of Ōmi[1] lived a poor old man. He sorely regretted never having been able to see the capital and decided to go for a visit. The very first thing that caught his eye as he walked down Fourth Avenue was a mirror, displayed among the myriad wares offered by numerous tradesmen.[2] The old man had no way of knowing that this kind of mirror had recently spread from Kumano and was commonly available in the capital, so he picked up the bright, shining round thing and examined it in wonder. When he peered into it, beautiful women and precious goods reflected back. Assuming that all this came from within the round thing, he told the merchant that he wanted to buy it. When the amused tradesman stated the price—a thousand pieces of gold—the man pulled out the money and bought it on the spot.[3]

On his return home, the old man wanted to show his wife and mother all the beautiful women and precious goods inside the round thing but decided that perhaps this was not an appropriate time. Instead, he hid it up deep within a four-legged trunk. His wife was watching, however, and her suspicions were aroused. She

waited until her husband was absent, then pulled it out and discovered a bright shining round object. She looked into it: there was a woman! "He's gone and brought back a woman, and now he's trying to hide her from me! How infuriating! I won't let him get away with this!" she thought angrily. Calling over his mother, she sobbed, "Look at this! He brought back a woman from the capital! How hateful of him!"

The man returned from the mountain to find his wife looking quite pale and strange. Tapping her knees, she trembled and shook back and forth. "If you think that you're going to keep that woman from the capital, how on earth do you plan to feed her? We just don't have the means! You should be ashamed of yourself, and at your age! How spiteful!" She cried and wailed and beat her breast.

No matter what he said, the man was unable to appease his wife's wrath. He was mortified that all the neighbors might be listening in and stood dejectedly in thought. "As long as I keep this round thing, the household will be in an uproar. That makes it my enemy, and I'll have to destroy it." He took out an old sword and swung at it, cutting it into pieces. His wife and mother ran off to parts unknown at the swishing of the blade.

The man feverishly hacked it to bits, and, just when he thought that he must have finally finished it off, he looked down and saw a number of individual faces. It had to be a demon! He was so terrified that his hair stood on end. Quickly he leaped into a threshing

sack, wiped the sweat from his brow, and took a deep breath. Should he sit it out? Or should he try for a sneak attack with a bow and feather-winged arrows? Either way, surely the demon had grown tired by now. Creeping up quickly and stealthily, he took a peek. There it was, glittering as brightly as ever.

The man gave up. At least his life and reputation were still intact. He withdrew from the battle and fled, but the thing seemed to follow after him, sparkling away, as he ran on and on, deeper and deeper into the mountains. Night fell, and he could no longer hear the cries of the nightingale. The only sounds that came to his ears were the whispering pines and the echoes of water flowing through the valley. When he finally came to his senses, he realized that he was exhausted and chilled to the bone.

Far off in a distant valley he saw a faint glimmer of light. Relying on it as a guide, he pushed through thorns and pampas grass until he reached the source. Nestled at the base of a cliff, set back in a grove of tall trees, was a kind of hut covered with moss. The man called out for help, and a woman of about forty, hair unbound and disheveled, suddenly appeared. "Ordinary people do not venture into this place," she said. "Tell me why you are here." The man explained that he had lost his way and needed to know the way home, then asked for shelter until daybreak. "If that's the case, then enter," she replied, and led him inside.

Seen from within, the dwelling was far too spacious to be called a simple hut. The rafters and pillars were black with smoke and so

coated with soot that they seemed to be lacquered. A bevy of beautiful women was moving around to the rear, and white mice frolicked nearby. The man marveled at all he saw. His hostess served him a snack, then said, "There are no men in this place, only women. It is called Hidden Village, or Kamegatani,[4] and is often blessed by the manifestation of the Chikubushima Benten.[5] The presence of a man marks a highly auspicious occasion. We must reward you with precious things." She added a pinch of gold dust to an elixir of immortality and bade him drink. She then told him to depart before dawn and never tell a soul of this place. He would find his way out if he followed the turns of the valley.

The man followed her instructions and arrived back at his own village. Summoning his wife and mother, he gave them the elixir to drink. They produced many children, became rich and respected, were blessed with numerous descendants, and flourished ever after.

NOTES

1. An area corresponding to present-day Shiga Prefecture.

2. Bronze mirrors have been used in Japan since antiquity. This was probably a copper mirror, which became widely used in medieval times and which may have been produced in the region of Kumano. Mercury-coated mirrors were first introduced by the Dutch at Nagasaki.

3. That a poor man should possess such a large sum of money is typical of the inconsistencies frequently appearing in otogi-zōshi. The *Shintōshū* version of this story has the man borrowing the money from friends.

4. Probably a corruption of *kami ga tani,* "valley of the gods," or *kagami ga tani,* "valley of mirrors."

5. Benten is a goddess known for her beauty. A shrine dedicated to her is located on Chikubushima, an island in the northeast corner of Lake Biwa.

A Tale of Brief Slumbers
Utatane no sōshi

The Japanese have traditionally held that dreams are as valid a reflection of reality as is waking consciousness. Much of premodern Japanese literature explores the dichotomy between "dream" and "reality," often concluding that dream is ultimately the truer of the two. *A Tale of Brief Slumbers* is based on the idea of courtship begun and pursued within the realm of dreams when reality offers no opportunity to meet.

This tale, however improbable, points to the dreary reality behind the daily lives of aristocratic women. Like the young lady in the story, these women were obliged by social convention to remain secluded and inactive, their long idle days punctuated only by the diversions of regular seasonal activities. It is not surprising that they should have seen the world of dreams as an attractive alternative to reality.

A Tale of Brief Slumbers combines romance and miracle tale in a lyrical narrative of aristocratic love. The story is a variation on the Japanese Cinderella motif, which features a neglected, beautiful, and motherless girl of high birth who ultimately is discovered by a handsome young nobleman, usually through divine assistance. It is written in a highly elliptic, indirect prose style similar to that of the earlier literary tradition of the romance, of which *The Tale of Genji* is the most well-known example. This style was considered an appropriately august and literarily sanctioned vehicle for conveying stories of the nobility and is common to otogi-zōshi centering on aristocrats and their concerns. The text contains numerous allusions, both overt and covert, to poetry and legends concerning the dream/reality dichotomy. Strong influence from *The Tale of Genji* is evident in the many references to that tale, particularly in the latter half, where the girl is likened to Tamakazura. The last scene is a kind of inversion of the last chapters of the *Genji,* in which Ukifune goes out boating with Niou, then later drowns herself, and, of course, the action of *A Tale of Brief Slumbers* takes place at the temple at which the *Genji* was supposedly written.

This translation is based on the text annotated by Tajima Kazuo, printed in *Muromachi monogatari shū,* vol. 1, ed. Ichiko Teiji et al. Shin Nihon koten bungaku taikei 54 (Tokyo: Iwanami shoten, 1989). The manuscript, in the collection of the National Historical Folk Museum (Kokuritsu rekishi minzoku hakubutsukan), is in illustrated scroll format and dates to the latter half of the fifteenth century. Although authorship has traditionally been ascribed to one Asukai Masachika me, a female member of a literarily active family, there has surfaced no evidence that might confirm this. The illustrations have been provided courtesy of the Museum of Fine Arts, Boston, which houses a scroll of the same title, almost identical to the one translated here.

Utatane ni
koishiki hito wo
miteshi yori
yume chō mono wa
tanomisometeki

In a brief slumber
I caught sight of my beloved,
and now I cling to
each passing dream.[1]

These words of the poet Ono no Komachi expressed but a trifling
fancy in comparison to the passion that rejects even life itself.
Among the many tales of long ago is one extraordinary account of
such a love.

The story I am about to tell occurred in the not-too-distant past.
There was once a prominent minister well regarded at court. Of his
many children born to several consorts, one son was Master of the
Crown Prince's Household; another younger son held the rank of
prelate and was head priest of Ishiyama Temple. The Minister had
but a single daughter, sister to the Prelate, whom he cherished
beyond measure. He considered sending her to serve at court and
had already begun the preparations for her presentation when he
realized that she would be surrounded by a bevy of imperial consorts and ladies of the bedchamber. In such an atmosphere, even if
she were to receive imperial favor, she would be subjected to fierce
jealousy, and he feared lest she become withdrawn and sink into
depression. As he vacillated over the decision, certain presentable
suitors called with offers to marry and care for her, but he was reluctant to give his precious daughter to anyone at all.

Soon the girl blossomed into the full flower of maidenhood and
radiated such an array of charms that she was a pleasure to behold.
Her father treated her with special consideration, inviting young
ladies of excellent qualities to serve her. At times she lived happily,
deriving amusement from the many diversions afforded by the
spring flowers and autumnal foliage. Other times, however, the
weight of her father's duties led him to neglect her, and, her
mother having passed away, the girl perforce spent long hours in
lonely idleness.

67

Near her rooms grew a late-blooming wild cherry tree, adorned with blossoms far outlasting those of other flowering trees. As the spring days slipped away, she found solace in these flowers and lamented their final descent to earth. One lonely afternoon, as the long rains gently fell and droplets ceaselessly pattered on the eaves, she left off her aimless plucking at the koto and lay down, falling off into a deep sleep.

Suddenly, it seemed that someone appeared before her, proffering a branch of flowing wisteria deeply fragrant despite the dew still clinging to it. Attached to the branch was a slip of paper tinted in the same pale lavender hue as the wisteria. Assuming that this lovely offering was a message from the Kamo Priestess,[2] the girl casually picked it up. In a man's hand was written:

Omoine ni	Yet more fleeting than a daydream
miru yume yori mo	from the slumbers of love—
hakanaki wa	the vision of another,
shiranu utsutsu no	a reality yet unknown.
yoso no omokage	

The traces of ink were well modulated and the hand remarkable, revealing that the poem had been written by no ordinary person. She gazed at it with admiration, her heart in turmoil, wondering who might have sent it. This was a most unexpected dream!

This vivid vision had been so beautiful and the traces of his brush so lovely that her heart was quite captivated, and she yearned to see more. She sat lost in bemused contemplation until night fell. Lamps were brought in, and she played at *go* with her attendant Chūnagon and nursemaid Ben. Though she tried to maintain interest in the game, she was wholly preoccupied by thoughts of the unknown man in that fleeting dream and overwhelmed by a sense of unreality. In a daze, she pulled over the movable screen to take a brief nap.

There at her side was a figure wearing a soft courtier's robe layered over a crimson robe and trousers of pale lavender lined with green. The color and quality of his dress were so elegant and his fragrance so profoundly penetrating that she was quite entranced. They lay together with an intimacy as of long association. When she cast a glance at his face, her heart throbbed wildly. So radiantly handsome and charming was he, possessed of such refinement and a host of appealing features, that he brought to mind the shining Prince Genji of tales of old. Indeed, the very sight of him led her to think that even a man could possess the proverbial hundred charms.[3] Mute in her agitation, tears streaming down, she tried to move away, but he grasped her hand and addressed her.

"The anguish of my love cannot but have moved you to pity—did you not even look at the faint traces of my brush? Your failure to respond caused me such distress that I was compelled to come. Do you not know the expression 'a slave to love?' The bonds linking a man and woman are not only of this life but are fated from past lives as well. So often in the past has unrequited longing led to terrible retribution! If you and I were to leave our love unconsummated in this world, it would wander aimlessly on the dark path to come. Would this not be a lamentable fate?"

He tearfully spoke on, though unable to pour out all that was in his heart. Somehow he seemed to know that she was not unmoved, though he could not possibly hear her response. All too soon there came the faint sound of the cock's call of dawn. "The cock must be well accustomed to the resentment of departing lovers," she heard him say dispiritedly.[4] Just one encounter could not possibly suffice for the full exchange of lovers' intimacies. Sensing something oppressing her, she looked up to see that the sun had risen high in the sky. With a sense of utter unreality, she arose, but was not at all herself.

How terribly confusing was this dream arisen from slumbers beneath the spring blossoms! It had always been said that, in a love dream, the object of yearning appeared in one's own dream, but she had also heard that a soul could wander afar to visit the dreams of the beloved,[5] as exemplified in the lines by Princess Shikishi, "the one I would see even in a dream."[6] What kind of dream had this been? Who had appeared before her? What unknown sender had offered these blossoms of affection? Should others realize that she was lying lovelorn in the shadows of the tree of laments, sleeves damp with tears, they would regard it as deeply sinful.[7]

When her lover Fujiwara no Norimichi ceased to call on her, Ko Shikibu passed long empty months in melancholy. Suddenly he came to visit, and she was beside herself with joy. When it came time for him to depart, she stitched a thread on the sleeve of his cloak as a memento. By daylight, however, she saw the thread caught in a tree in the garden and realized that he had not really come. Her own excess of longing had summoned before her the image sheltered in her heart.[8]

Who was it that loved her both in dream and in reality? Although there was no way to communicate her longing to him, her heart remained in turmoil. "How did I sleep that night such as to see him?" she wondered as she lay on her lonely bed.[9] Her own fragrance wafting up served as the only reminder of that vision. She so yearned for him, and dwelled so constantly on him, that presently she completely lost her ability to distinguish reality from dream. The thought of anything else—even things she had previ-

ously liked—was distasteful to her. As time passed, she weakened and became increasingly distraught, unable so much as to glance at food. Deeply concerned, her father and attendants offered prayers and commissioned services for her recovery. Day and night the halls were filled with the commotion of rituals and sutra recitations, but she remained sunken in her own reveries. That her father should worry so on her behalf became to her a source of further anguish, and she grew even worse.

Shocked to hear of her condition, her brother the Prelate came to conduct services on her behalf. Some hope lay in the particularly effective vow of salvation for all sentient beings made by the Savior Kannon of Ishiyama; there had been much talk of the miracles she[10] performed. He promised that the girl would make a pilgrimage to Ishiyama if her condition were sufficiently relieved to permit the journey. To everyone's vast relief, her health improved, most probably owing to the innumerable prayers on her behalf.

Soon she was making hurried preparations for a journey to Ishiyama. She chose to travel without carriage or fanfare, limiting her

retinue to Chūnagon, her nurse, and four or five close attendants, for her petition was just as weighty as that of Lady Tamakazura, who had traveled far on foot to Hatsuse Temple.[11]

When she arrived, she was impressed by the singular beauty of the place. From the foot of the cliffs stretched a moon-bathed expanse of rippling waves; the cliffs were covered by deep layers of moss—untold aeons must have passed since they were mere pebbles.[12] The ancient garden was suffused with the silence of another world, and all the hardships of her journey were forgotten as she gazed at it. She prayed fervently and prostrated herself in supplication. Entreating that her many afflictions be vanquished, intoning loudly the prayer, "Thy great vow is as deep as the seas,"[13] she paid homage with all her soul.

Late at night, she finally completed her worship. The room adjoining her own was said to have sheltered Murasaki Shikibu when writing *The Tale of Genji,* and the girl was curious to see this unusual place. Suddenly she heard a refined voice from within. It seemed that a certain general of the left was summoning a middle captain. Then the voice of the Middle Captain responded.

"Why did you come here to pray when the annual court appointment ceremonies[14] were nigh, when you had pressing obligations both public and private? I cannot but wonder why you have wet your sleeves in these autumnal dews to come here. It defies all reason! You have not told me the least thing about why we are here, and it pains me to feel such a gulf between us. It seems that you are atoning for some sin you have committed—please tell me," he entreated sadly.

"Well, you know that one should not speak of dreams at night,"[15] replied the General, "but you are so concerned, and there is no longer any point in concealing it. I have entrusted the Buddha with my prayers for a clear resolution to my longings."

His manner of speaking was precisely that of the man who had visited her dreams. Her heart was thrown into turmoil, and she was desperate for a glimpse of him. Her attendants were already fast asleep, fatigued from the long journey. The lamp had been extinguished, and light shone brightly from the next room. Peering in through the crack in the door, she saw an elegant man dressed in hunting garb sitting forlornly. He was identical in every respect to the man of her dreams. Thinking that she must be dreaming again, she listened on, suppressing the dark storms in her heart.

"In China and in Japan, people have been guided by dreams, one seeking on Fugan Plain,[16] another on the shores of Akashi.[17] In these and other cases, their dreams have coincided with reality. At the end of the third month of last year, I received a poem, apparently from a woman, attached to a lovely branch of wisteria:

Tanome tada	I wake to find
omoiawasuru	our tryst but a reverie—
omoi ne no	would that dreams too
utsutsu ni kaeru	come back to life.
yume mo koso are	

Ever since then, we have visited each other nightly for almost two years. We have vowed the eternally fresh passion of intertwined branches of two trees and the ever-constant love of two birds sharing one wing.[18] Throughout my service at court and in the privacy of my own affairs, through the beauty of the changing seasons, I have been living solely in the hope that my dreams might be realized. Consumed with the thought of it, I could attend to nothing else; I am no longer myself and have weakened in body and spirit. I have rested all hope on this pilgrimage."

The girl was profoundly moved to hear him alternately laughing and crying as he poured out his tale of love and sadness. This indeed was the dream she had seen and the reality behind it! She desperately longed to pull open the sliding door that separated them and to converse of their nightly pledges. Yet such forwardness was inappropriate for a woman, and she was forced to repress the urge.

She was at the end of her wits. Those ephemeral dreams had rendered her unable to forget him; now she had heard the same tale about dreams of love and seen the same face of her dreams. All this had come to an end as empty as the open sky, for there was no way to bridge the gap between them, even for a moment. She had no way of predicting his reaction should she burst in and pour out her raging emotions, so she was unable to speak out or go to his side. For her, this stolen glimpse must be their only encounter. Her only recourse lay in becoming a fisherwoman[19] in the waters, trusting that the ever-flowing currents of love would unite them in the world to come. Thus she bravely resolved to die.

After her mother's death, she had relied solely on her father and looked to him for protection; he in turn had loved her dearly. Should she commit the grave sin of predeceasing her parent, somber skies must darken the path she would tread in the hereafter.[20] As he awaited her return on the morrow, he would be unaware that the brief full tide of her life would soon recede—with what sorrow would he receive the tidings, and how he would mourn! Still her resolution wavered not. Sadly, she remembered those who had served her for so long and her friends at court—the Kamo Priestess, the Empress, the various imperial princes and princesses. Regrettably, shallow rumors would cling to her unhappy name in the wake of her death. Numerous considerations gave her pause, but her

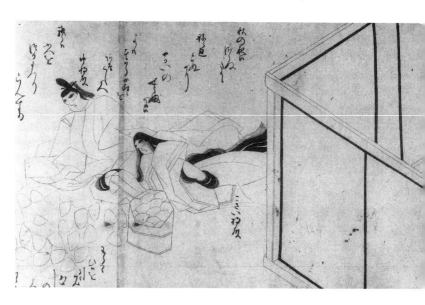

resolve was strengthened by the prospect of meeting her beloved in the world to come. She lit the lamp and wrote a letter to her father, her eyes so blurred by tears that she was barely able to see. "Do not grieve. Alas, the dews on the young clover of spring[21] are fleeting, yet all must die in the end."

Dawn finally broke. Chūnagon and the others read the sutras, the girl's own faintly whispered prayers barely audible. As her attendants admired the dawn breaking over the waters and mountains, she reflected on their grief should they discover the slightest dewdrop of her heart's intentions. It was indeed sad, but she had been granted a glimpse of the reality behind her dream vision and the knowledge that his feelings mirrored hers. This had to be a manifest token of the Kannon's expedient means, a trustworthy guide to the world to come that lent her courage to face the end with serenity. Hoping that the sin of dying before her parent might prove to be a kind of inverse karma,[22] she prayed that she and her beloved might share a lotus leaf in perfect nuptial harmony in the Pure Land. Though this was her own heart's desire, it was nonetheless very sad.

Her party hastened to depart before the sun rose higher. Her brother's wetnurse, now bent with age, lived close to the nearby Seta Bridge. She had implored them to come visit, saying, "I live so near to where you will be passing. It won't do to let this rare opportunity go to waste . . . if I could only see you. Please come— then you can continue your journey by carriage." For one with intentions such as hers, visiting a place near the water provided a good pretext.

Her heart composed, the girl walked calmly as a lamb to slaughter,[23] yet, the closer she drew to the bridge, the more foreboding the water seemed. What retribution from another life had led her to the depths of this watery grave? Now that the moment of death was on her, she imagined her father's terrible desolation after his only daughter had departed the world before him. Among the many examples of sad events that flooded her mind was the line of verse, "I know not where I go in the hereafter . . . ,"[24] and she was obliged to brush away the torrent of tears coursing down her face lest someone remark them. In the middle of the bridge, she paused, wavered indecisively, then leaped into the waters below.

"What has she done!" screamed her nurse in shock, standing transfixed in utter horror. Unable to restrain her tears, lacking even the presence of mind to jump in after her, her only thought was somehow to rescue her mistress, and she screamed for help at the top of her lungs.

Just then there appeared an elegant boat bearing a number of gentlemen dressed in hunting costume, who wondered at her hysterical sobbing. Overjoyed to see them, the nurse wildly screamed out, "Someone has just jumped in. Can you help?" stamping her feet in the frenzy of her emotion. Moved by pity for her, they resolutely let down some men familiar with the ways of the water, who dragged up the girl.

That the girl should be rescued from the watery depths was indeed a true witness to the message of the Lotus Sutra.[25] Miraculously, her robes bore not a trace of moisture, as if they had been dry for many a long year.

The boat bore none other than the General, who, having completed his seven days of prayer, was on his way home. After the lady had been safely bundled aboard, the General regarded her closely. She was not yet twenty years old, charming and innocent, with striking eyes and features that brought to mind a far-off white-wreathed mountain cherry in the misty dawn light. Her face was modestly averted, and her abundant hair spilled down luxuriantly, nary a wisp astray, filled with the dewy grace of a willow.[26] He felt that his customary dream was but an ephemera compared to this glowing reality. They spoke together without tiring, as if they had known each other for years. One might expect that a woman of such tender years would be embarrassed at having been pulled up in this manner, but she felt not a trace of reserve, for this was the same man dear to her in her dream life.

The love they shared was so strong that it flourished even in the darkness of a jet-black dream; how much more now that they were able to meet in reality! The revered Kannon had led them to realize their long-standing karmic bond. They lived happily ever after, wanting for nothing, assisted by the excellence of the reign, and their legendary prosperity extended even to their children and grandchildren.[27]

I should like to write on further, but I intended to tell only the story of a couple brought together in a dream through the manifestation of the Savior Bodhisattva's vow, and I shall leave the embellishment to another. To ramble on further would be a waste of ink, so I shall put aside my brush.

NOTES

1. *Kokinshū* no. 553, by the famed poetess Ono no Komachi.

2. As later becomes apparent, the girl is on friendly terms with several members of the imperial family. The Kamo Priestess was always selected from offspring of the imperial or princely families.

3. A common description of female beauty, based on a description of the legendary beauty Yang Kuei Fei in "The Song of Unending Sorrow": "If she but turned her head and smiled, there were cast a hundred smiles, / And the powder and paint of the Six Palaces faded into nothing" (Birch, ed., *Anthology of Chinese Literature,* p. 266).

4. It was customary for lovers to depart at dawn, which was signaled by the cock's crow.

5. The text is distinguishing between two kinds of dream appearances: the love dream *(omoine)*, in which one falls asleep yearning for another and consequently dreams of that person, and the case in which one's spirit leaves one's sleeping body and appears in the dreams of another.

6. *Shinkokinshū* no. 1124: "Yume nite mo / miyuran mono wo / nage-kitsutsu / uchinuru yoi no / sode no keshiki wa" (Lamenting for the one / I would see even in a dream / my sleeves of evening / drenched with tears).

7. This passage is somewhat unclear, particularly the line stating that, should others see her, it would be "deeply sinful" *(tsumibukaki)*. It may be that the term is used weakly, in the sense of "undesirable"; otherwise, it is difficult to see how the girl's sad plight would be all that sinful, unless, of course, she had been pledged already to another.

8. This legend of Ko Shikibu, the daughter of the famed poetess Izumi Shikibu, is recounted in several sources, among them episode 26 of the *Ima monogatari (Tales of the Present)*.

9. A reference to *Kokinshū* no. 516: "Yoi yoi ni / makura sadamen / kata mo nashi / ika ni neshi yo ka / yume ni mienu" (Night after night / I shift my pillow around / how did I sleep that night / that I saw him in my dreams?).

10. The Kannon was frequently envisioned as female. See, e.g., the description of the Ishiyama Kannon in *The Tale of Ikago*.

11. In *The Tale of Genji*, the orphaned Tamakazura makes a pilgrimage to petition the gods of Hatsuse for help in locating her father. At Hatsuse, she meets her mother's former maidservant, now in the household of Genji; thereafter her fortunes change for the better.

12. See n. 32 to *The Little Man*.

13. From chap. 25 of the Lotus Sutra, which describes the limitless compassion of the Bodhisattva Kannon.

14. *Tsukasameshi no jimoku*, an annual three-day-long ceremony held in the fall, at which court appointments were conferred.

15. Apparently, contemporary superstition had it that speaking of one's dreams at night was unlucky.

16. Legend has it that Emperor Yin, founder of the Shang dynasty, was led by a dream to discover a loyal minister living there.

17. In the *Tale of Genji*, the old priest of Akashi is bidden in a dream to seek someone on the shores of Akashi. There he finds Genji, who subsequently weds his daughter.

18. See the ending of *The Little Man*, in which love is described in the same terms borrowed from "The Song of Unending Sorrow."

19. A reference to a poem in the *Kokin waka rokujō* anthology: "Kono yo ni te / kimi wo mirume no / kata karaba / konyo no ama to narite / kazuken" (If in this world I may not reap / the grasses of seeing you / then I shall become a fisherwoman / in the one to come). The first oblique reference to her intention to drown herself.

20. Parents were thought to guide offspring down the dark path after death.

21. The message incorporates a pun on *ko hagi*, "young/child" and "bush clover," retained in English as "of spring" (offspring).

22. *Gyakuen*, lit., "reverse karma," here refers to the doctrine that religious ends can be achieved even through ostensibly wrong causes.

23. *Hitsuji no ayumi*, lit., "the paces of a sheep (to its death)," an expression derived from the Nirvāna Sutra, similar to the English "a lamb to slaughter."

24. See n. 20 above. An allusion to a poem written on her sickbed by Ko Shikibu no Naishi, daughter of Izumi Shikibu: "Ika ni semu / ikubeki kata mo omoezu / oya ni sakidatsu / michi wo shiraneba" (What shall I do? / I know not where I go / along the path I walk / before my parents). In *Kokon chōmonjū*, vol. 5, no. 175; also referred to in *Shasekishū*, vol. 5, no. 9, and *Mumyō zōshi*.

25. In the Kannon chapter of the Lotus Sutra, it is stated that, if one is swept off by a great river and calls on the Kannon, he shall find a shallow place.

26. A metaphor of female beauty, derived from "The Song of Unending Sorrow."

27. In the Japanese text, their prosperity is likened to that of "Fujinoura," a reference to the chapter of the same name in *The Tale of Genji*, which describes the full flowering of Genji's fortunes.

The Tale of Ikago
Ikago monogatari

The Tale of Ikago presents a fascinating view of the gentrification of the warrior. Having achieved political power, these rough, unlettered fighters from the countryside turned their attentions to the acquisition of its trappings, diligently learning poetry and the mechanics of poetry composition. Here, the fierce governor puts his newly acquired knowledge to coercive use in a "poetry battle" at which his underling, an illiterate samurai, is at a distinct disadvantage.

This story exhibits so many features common to otogi-zōshi that it may well be characterized as a paradigmatic example of the genre. The basic plot is derived from a miracle tale, versions of which appear in the *Konjaku monogatari shū,* vol. 16, no. 18, and the *Hasedera reigenki,* vol. 2, no. 20.[1] It has been expanded and fleshed out beyond the usual scope of the setsuwa genre through such devices of narrative expansion as the travel account *(michiyuki),* poeticized prose, dialogue, and narratorial explication.

The Tale of Ikago features a host of themes common to medieval short prose: poetry is valorized, religious dedication and supplication are proved effective, a popular deity protects and defends her adherents, a defeated malefactor realizes the error of his ways, and simple virtue and sincerity receive their just reward. Though such a high degree of didacticism might tend to become heavy handed, the message is made palatable by numerous touches of light humor and pathos, which serve to humanize the narrative.

This translation is based on the unannotated text transcribed from an unillustrated bound manuscript in the Tenri Library collection, printed in *Muromachi jidai monogatari taisei* (2:185-192). There remain only two extant copies of this story; the other, dated 1751, has never been reproduced in typeset.

Once in a certain reign and time, there lived a district official of Ikago in the province of Ōmi. This man had a most wonderful wife: she was not only uncommonly beautiful but also gentle and kind. She would gaze at the beauties of each passing season and, her heart stirred by the spring blossoms and autumnal foliage, would recite poetry of old. She was adept at several musical instruments, wrote in a delightful hand, and was even accomplished in needlework. Although men from all around were smitten by her charms, she scrupulously observed proper wifely conduct, followed the five virtues, and never once engaged in any kind of flirtatious behavior. It was often remarked that her virtue knew no peers.

The Governor of the province had heard this woman's praise sung so frequently that he decided somehow to make her his own. Alas, since the mute woods of decorum forbade direct address, he was obliged to send a barrage of letters over the linked bridge to her shores. Yet it mattered not to the wife whether her suitor was of high or humble rank: she would see no one but her husband and accepted no such addresses, leaving his letters to accumulate untouched. The Governor was deeply smitten, his heart adrift in the turbulent waves of an unseen bay. There seemed to be no way to tell her of his feelings. Determined to have her at all costs, he devised a scheme to make her his own.[2]

First, a messenger bearing a summons to the Governor's residence was dispatched to the husband. The surprised husband wondered what was afoot, but hurried to obey. When he announced himself at the mansion, he was received far more cordially than ever before. "Of all the people in this province, I consider you the wisest of all. I've called you here in order to have you speak frankly of all things, both past and present," said the Governor, though he meant not a word of it. He plied the hapless man with rare delicacies and wine. Overwhelmed with delight, the husband drank freely and spoke openly of everything that came to mind. He was moved to drunken tears by the high esteem with which his humble self was regarded, and his senses began to reel. At this point, the

Governor posed a question. "No matter what I ask of you, would you obey me?"

"Ah, you speak of my loyalty, yet seem not to believe it," replied the husband. "You have been entrusted with the rule of the province by commission of the Emperor. Were I to disobey you, I would be flouting the imperial will. If I disregarded the law of the land in such a way, I could never hold up my head anywhere in the realm. Please say whatever you like."

"Well, then, let us have a contest," said the Governor. "You must not be intimidated, but do the best you can. If you win, I will divide my domain in two and award you half, to rule just as you like. If I win, however, you must deliver to me your wife."

Withdrawing an inkstone from his writing desk, he wrote down some words, sealed the paper shut, and placed it inside a lacquer box decorated with pines, birds, and a fishing boat. He shut the box, pressed his seal on it, and pushed it over to the husband.

"You are forbidden to open this. Inside are the first three lines of a poem; you are to compose two final lines that match its spirit. Take the box home, but do not look inside. Return in seven days with your response. If the two verses fit together, I will forthwith give you half my domain—just leave the formalities to me. If the poem reads badly, though, your wife is mine."[3]

The husband's heart skipped a beat. He was no god, but a simple soul born and bred of the country earth and deep grasses, a man who knew only songs of planting and harvesting. He could never respond to those lines, even if he knew what they were! To make matters worse, the Governor had sealed the paper without showing or even telling him what it said. His lord had taken advantage of his drunken state to extract an unfair pledge. How could he give up his wife to another when throughout their years together she had remained within their humble reed fence and never once left his side?

"I am so coarse that I don't even know how many syllables a poem ought to contain. How can I possibly win?" he objected.

But the Governor assumed a stern expression and said, "How can you make light of something you have already solemnly sworn?" Indeed, not even a chariot equipped with four horses could retrieve the foolish words[4] of compliance that the poor man had let escape. Too cowed to look up at his lord's fierce bearded countenance, he returned in a daze, weeping all the way home.

At home his wife was waiting uneasily, though unaware of what was transpiring. Quite a few hours had passed since her husband had been unexpectedly summoned to call on the Governor. It was now late in the spring night, and the drifting clouds obscuring the moon filled her with foreboding. In an attempt to soothe her troubled spirits, she plucked at the koto near her pillow and tried to play a melody, but the middle string was weak, and the tone was bad. She set it aside:

Haru no yo no	Hazy moon of a spring night
narai ni kasumu	so easily bemisted—
tsukikage mo	now completely eclipsed
itodo namida ni	by a veil of tears.
kumori hatenuru	

With a sigh, she spread out her robes and lay down.

It was not until well after the nearby temple bell had tolled the midnight hour that her husband finally returned. Weeping copiously, he paced outside their bedchamber, one hand holding the box, the other pressed against his brow. His wife was taken aback. What could have happened? Though her heart was pounding, she summoned her composure and said, "This weeping and wailing would frighten even the Goddess of Crying Pond![5] If you have something to say, tell me immediately!"

"You wouldn't speak so harshly if you knew what has happened! For all these years, you have not left my side even for a moment. We have openly shared both grief and joy in affectionate harmony, but now our long-flourishing love is doomed to wither and die. In just five or six days, our life together will be at an end. It's no wonder that I'm crying!" he told her tremulously, eyes fixed on her face, once again letting forth a shower of tears.

This was all most unexpected. "Why do you say that all is lost?"

she responded. "I might understand if I heard the circumstances. Quickly, tell me!" Weeping, he told her everything that had occurred, starting with the Governor's hearty welcome.

His wife paused to think, then said, "Listen to me carefully. You must follow your lord's orders and try to come up with an answer. If you fail, it would be due to karma from a previous life, and you would have to accept it. But you needn't be so stupid as to accept defeat without even trying!

"Think about it: ever since the days when the god Susano-ō composed the first poem,[6] the profound path of poetry has demanded far more than a mere knowledge of the correct number of syllables a verse should contain. What's more, even the nobility, who are well known for their poetic skill, couldn't possibly supply a fitting ending for a verse they hadn't even seen. In tales of the past, it is written that Narihira inscribed on a cup lines about crossing a stream in order to complete a verse about reuniting at Joining Hill Barrier. However, this was possible only because he had seen the first lines, enabling him to match the two halves perfectly, like the upper and lower sancta of a shrine.[7]

"It's a shame that you fell into the Governor's trap, but we can't do anything about that now. No mere foolish mortal has the power to solve this problem—you must rely on the buddhas and bodhi-sattvas, who have compassion for all living creatures. If you petition in all sincerity, they may reverse your grim fate. Of them all, the compassionate Kannon in particular has vowed to save the world, alleviate suffering, and provide relief to all. There is no need to go far away: the Kannon at Ishiyama Temple[8] is well known for the miracles she performs. Go there and pray devoutly. If your karma is too strong and you receive no sign of her mercy, then we must leave this domain. Together you and I shall hide ourselves somewhere deep in the mountains or in the dark recesses of a valley, there to dwell simply, true to our eternal vows of fidelity. Come now! It's supposed to be the husband who admonishes the wife, not the other way around! What a hopeless fellow you are!" she chided.

Her husband finally regained his senses. He stopped weeping and decided to follow her advice. Beginning that very day, he purified the house and had everyone, even the servants, commence ritual dietary abstinence. Day and night he lay prostrate in prayer facing the direction of Ishiyama Temple. On the evening of the third day, he washed his hair[9] and set out at dawn.

As he journeyed, the turbulence of Peace River brought thoughts of how very hard it was to make one's way through this life. Mirror Mountain presented a clouded image, and the long bridge at Seta extended his despair, while Joining Hill Barrier brought to mind the difficulty of linking two halves of a poem. Finally, he reached Ishiyama, where he prayed to the Kannon.

"Please give me a sign that you uphold your vow of compassion! Oh Savior Bodhisattva, would that you bestow the benefit of your grace, reveal the entire poem, melt the hateful mien of the fearsome Governor, and grant me half the domain! Help me remain with my wife and observe our undying vows in this life and the one to come, until she and I are reborn in the land of the Buddha, when we shall behold your countenance!"

Tears dampened his sleeve as he fervently prayed, maintaining his vigil throughout the night. What with all his troubles of late, the rigors of his fast, and the fatigue of the journey, he fell into a dead stupor, oblivious to the tolling of the late night bell and the clanging of the morning chimes. The cock's crow brought no sign that his prayers had been heard. The Governor had threatened him . . . his wife was to be torn from his side . . . he would be terribly shamed and driven off . . . and he was powerless to stop it.

Finally, the sound of his own lamentations woke him from his dazed dreams. His entire body was drenched in sweat, and he was at the end of his endurance. He heard the clatter of flower basins, and a group of monks come to offer incense and water laughed at his sleepy swollen face. Mortified, he leaped up without a word of explanation and fled the sanctuary. A crowd of people had come to worship that day; several of the returning pilgrims approached him with curiosity to inquire the cause of his distress. "It's nothing at all," he replied to each.

Just as he was passing through the main gate, there appeared an elegant lady with a pale radiant face, garbed in a light lavender robe brocaded in deep purple, a dark cloak lined in white, and a veiled hat. Three or four female attendants trailed behind her. She too asked why he was in such a state. He felt the urge to confess that all his prayers had come to no avail, but instead denied having any troubles and told her that he hailed from Ikago.

"You must be worried about something. Please tell me," she said. Suddenly he realized that it was difficult indeed to predict the means employed by the Kannon's perfect wisdom: it could appear in any one of thirty-three manifestations. Even if she were not a divine messenger, however, the mere fact that the wind had brushed their sleeves at the same instant signaled a bond between them, and so her sympathy must be sincere.

He related everything that had happened, concluding, "and so I prayed to the bodhisattva to alleviate my suffering, but I must have slipped through the net of her all-encompassing vow. I have no recourse but to return home."

The lady drew nearer. "Why didn't you say so? It's such a simple request. Tell him that the poem ends thus: 'yield no seaweed, yet dear she is to me.' "

The man was overjoyed. "Please tell me your name and destination! I'd like to demonstrate my eternal gratitude!"

"Even the grasses of Musashi Plain are named but provisionally. How could I have a name?" She began to leave. "Occasionally I reside at the eastern end of the worship hall. You did well to come to me," she added with a smile, bathing him in the radiance of her face and fragrance of her robes. She moved off toward the hall and disappeared into the morning mist.

"The Kannon has deigned to rescue me!" he realized. Praying and muttering to himself the lines of poetry, he walked homeward, glancing back repeatedly at the temple until the roof tiles were eclipsed from sight.

At home, his wife had been gazing out at the water and reciting poetry in an attempt to calm her troubled spirit. She waited by the gate with a prayer on her lips and, as soon as her spouse appeared, eagerly inquired, "What happened? Did you receive a sign?"

"If one but places his trust in the buddhas, they fail not to respond," he answered reverently. Once inside, he told her all that had happened. The wife was so happy that she cried aloud and wept unceasingly. He repeated the lines he had heard, and they seemed to have an appropriately poetic cadence. She carefully wrote them down on a thin sheet of green paper, sealed it, and pressed it to her forehead in gratitude. Urashima Tarō may have met with misfortune when he opened his jeweled box,[10] but what evil could befall them when this was opened? Relying on the power of the Buddha's vow, she passed it to her husband.

On the evening of the seventh day, he went to the Governor's residence and announced himself. "There is so much at stake that I scarcely know what will become of it all, but I have brought an ending for the poem."

The excited Governor called together all the prominent local warriors and householders. He was filled with a sense of delightful anticipation. How pitiful it would be for the district official to lose his wife in this amusing verbal joust! The man could not possibly win unless the upper and lower links matched perfectly. Soon the official entered, and the Governor greeted him. "So, you managed to come back after all!"

"Listen, everyone," he announced. "If the meaning and diction of these lines match, I will bestow on this man half my domain. If not, he is to give me his wife. Such is the agreement we made. In order that there be no mistake, I'll want you all to act as witnesses." He complacently stroked his beard.

Praying to the Kannon, agonizing lest he had incorrectly recalled the verse, the trembling husband handed over the box and watched the Governor break the seal.

"I shall commence with my lines," said the Governor, and he read:

Ōmi naru	How can this be?
Ikago no umi no	The waters of Ikago
ika nareba	in the province of Ōmi

Then he opened the second sheet of paper and read out:

| mirume mo naki ni | yield no seaweed, |
| hito no koishiki | yet dear she is to me. |

Transfixed with admiration, he and the assembled company gasped. The amazed Governor called the man forward and questioned him repeatedly how he had ever come up with a response. "In my desperation, I relied on the Kannon at Ishiyama Temple to provide the response," was the only reply.

At this, even the savage heart of the Governor was tamed. "Indeed, nothing is possible save through the power of the buddhas!" he thought. Calling the crowd to order, he announced, "From this moment on, I divide my domain in two. You are to govern your half as you see fit." The husband was reluctant to accept such an award, but the Governor said, "I am a warrior, and it is against my code of honor to break my word. Such a thing would be shameful. It was I who proposed this wager; should I be false to it, I would fear the gods' wrath." And the Governor wrote down an official order of items to be granted to the husband: fifty-four rolls of assorted cloths, a large sword, one hundred gold coins, a horse and saddle, and other goods. "From this day hence, you are master of half the domain," he announced, offering a toast. Even he was delighted at the outcome.

His good name now secure, the husband returned home, where everyone from his wife to the most humble servant was overjoyed. He governed justly, his subjects prospered, his household flourished, and he was blessed with the finest son and daughter in the land. The couple's bliss grew manifold, and they were limitlessly happy.

All this was due to an exemplary wife's advice to trust and sincerely pray to the Kannon. As a result, the manifestation of the Kannon blessed the husband with compassion and boundless sympathy. In acknowledgment of the great favor the Kannon had shown him, he had regular services conducted at Ishiyama Temple, and his descendants continue the practice to this day.

If one inquires into the meaning of the poem, it may be understood as follows. The locale of the events was the district of Ikago in the province of Ōmi. The phrase *ika nareba* [how can this be?] plays on the place name *Ikago* and links the first half of the verse with the second, which speaks of wonder at being in love with a person as yet unseen. The sea of Ōmi is a freshwater lake, so it contains none of the various seaweeds gathered by fisherfolk. This notion is worked into the second link, *mirume mo naki ni* [no seaweed/never seen].[11] It is no wonder that this one poem caused the Governor's fierce heart to soften. He was so impressed by the power of the Buddha that he commenced religious practices for his own salvation.

With the help of the buddhas, the couple's love grew ever stronger. They created a splendid household, followed the path of the Buddha, and entered paradise in the life to come.

Even deep love for another can be a means to salvation and create favorable karma. One can enter the Pure Land through many gates, for there are innumerable means devised to help living beings. It is indeed awe inspiring!

NOTES

1. For a partial translation of the *Konjaku monogatari shū*, see Marian Ury, *Tales of Times Now Past: Sixty-two Stories from a Medieval Japanese Collection* (Berkeley: University of California Press, 1979). For a discussion of the *Hasedera reigenki*, see Yoshiko Dykstra, "Tales of the Compassionate Kannon: The Hasedera Kannon Genki," *Monumenta Nipponica* 31:2 (Summer 1976).

2. Like major portions of *The Errand Woman*, this entire paragraph is couched in highly poetic phrases of which the English translation is but a prosaic approximation. The "mute woods," *Iwade no mori*, creates a pun on the place name and *iwade*, "not to speak." The linked bridge refers to *Mama no tsugibashi*, a well-known poetic locale.

3. Joint poetry composition was a common poetic practice that reached its zenith in the demanding art of linked verse *(renga)*. The object was to compose lines that complemented the diction and spirit of those preceeding it, so as to create alternating verses of 5–7–5 and 7–7 syllables.

4. From Confucius' *Analects*.

5. Nakisawame no kami, said to have been born from the tears shed by the god Izanagi at the death of his consort Izanami.

6. The first poem in the *Kojiki,* popularly thought to have been the first ever composed.

7. The story has mistakenly reversed the order of the poetic lines. The original anecdote is recounted in episode 69 of *The Tales of Ise.*

8. Ishiyama Temple is in the same province of Ikago, present-day Shiga Prefecture. Murasaki Shikibu is said to have written *The Tale of Genji* while staying at the temple. (See *A Tale of Brief Slumbers.*) This association with literary genius may be why the husband makes his supplications there.

9. An act of ritual purification.

10. In the legend of Urashima Tarō, also recounted in an otogi-zōshi of the same title, the hero instantly ages when he opens a box given him by the daughter of the Dragon King.

11. The origin of this poem is uncertain, although the poetic conceits it employs are relatively common.

The Tale of the Brazier

Hioke no sōshi

The plot of *The Tale of the Brazier* hinges on an old woman's jealousy of her husband's beloved—in this case, not another woman, but a warm and comforting brazier that keeps him company through long chilly nights. The bulk of the narrative, however, consists of a verbal battle in which the combatants employ canonical wisdom, poetic allusions, and literary precedents in order to justify their respective positions. Their dialogue mimics the *mondō,* a medieval pedagogical and literary question-and-response form seen in nō, poetic treatises, and the Zen communication between master and disciple.

Poetry, traditionally considered the most hallowed of all arts, figures prominently in the couple's discourse. In the famed preface to the *Kokinshū* poetry anthology, poetry is invested with a number of quasi-magical properties, including softening relations between the sexes. This is precisely the function it serves within the story: each speaker recites poetry in defense of his or her position, and the narrative culminates with a poem from *The Tale of Genji* that leads them to marital reconciliation and spiritual dedication. The religiously inspired note concluding the story leads the reader to see it retrospectively as a kind of sermon about attachment and jealousy.

This translation is based on the text of an illustrated printed booklet *(tanrokubon)* in the Akagi bunko collection, printed without annotations in *Muromachi jidai monogatari taisei* (11:13–24). Illustrations are courtesy of the Tenri Library, which has an identical booklet. For information helpful to creating several of the annotations, I am indebted to Tokuda Kazuo's "Hioke no sōshi no kōzō to hōhō," in *Mukashi banashi to bungaku,* ed. Nomura Jun'ichi, Nihon mukashi banashi shūsei 5 (Tokyo: Meisaku shuppan, 1985).

Long ago there lived an old man and woman in a poor thatched hut far off in a small country hamlet. Each evening the old man would sit at the side of their wooden brazier, and each morning he would compose poetry about it. The old woman burned with jealousy whenever she heard him intoning verses such as this:

Samushiro ni   If not for the brazier,
koromo katashiku   who would give me solace
yo mo sugara   as alone I pass the nights
hioke narade wa   on a single sleeve of my robe?[1]
tare ka tanoman

Each night he would fondly snuggle up to the brazier and fawn over it. His irate wife repeatedly warned him that she would smash it to bits if he persisted, but he paid her no heed.

One day, while the old man was out collecting kindling to stoke the brazier, his wife picked up an axe and confronted her rival.

"Now you're going to hear how selfishly you've behaved for the past ten years," she told it. "All the time I've been living here, drawing the water, picking the crops, and running the household, you've been lollygagging with him. During the day, you never let him leave your side, and at night, when by all rights he should be sleeping with me, you nestle close to his bosom. It's absolutely galling, the way he sings you songs, reads you poetry, and holds you so dear to his heart! And when I try to cuddle up with him, he tosses me aside—oh, many are the nights I've wished only to die! But, when I thought it over, I realized that, the longer I live, the greater the chance that I'll receive heaven's blessing. As they say, even a blind turtle has a chance of finding his way to Mount Hōrai![2] I've put up with you for a long time! A man is allowed to strike down his wife's seducer on the spot, so say your prayers now, brazier!"

She swung the axe high and brought it down hard, splitting the brazier in two. As her husband had so often averred in his poetry, it was a truly remarkable brazier: red-colored blood gushed from it and spattered everywhere.

Soon the old man returned from the mountain and caught sight
of his brazier. "How could such a thing have happened?" he wondered. "I'll bet the old lady knows something about it!" Grabbing
a stick close at hand, he thrashed her soundly, berating and accus-
ing her all the while.

The old woman looked up through her tears. "Listen to my side
of it, old man! Even a stepchild has a valid point of view! When
you were sixteen and I fifteen, we became husband and wife, and
have been together seventy years since. In my younger days, all
sorts of men from miles around—priests, mendicants, young lords
—would get that gleam in their eyes over me, and words of love
would fall readily from their lips. They would beckon to me, tug at
my sleeves, pull at my hem, and carry on, begging for my attention. But I wasn't swayed in the least, not even once. Never has my
flesh known the touch of any man but you! I thought that our
bonds were as strong as the likes of Yūshi and Hakuyō of old
China.[3] You heartless old man! I couldn't bear the way you cherished that brazier, without once looking my way! From this day
forth, I relinquish all the property to you. Please release me from
this marriage—I can fend for myself."[4]

The old man heard her out and snorted derisively. "What a miserable heart you have! Your sins are grave indeed; even the gods,
buddhas, and Three Treasures[5] must deplore you. Even if you were
virtuous, though, it is no easy matter for a woman to aspire to Buddhahood, as the Five Hindrances and the Three Duties attest. I will
explain to you each of the Five Hindrances in this world.

"The origins of the Five Hindrances are explained in the fifth
book of the Lotus Sutra. First, a woman cannot become a Brahma
king, second, she cannot become the god Sakra, third, she cannot
become the king Mara, fourth, she cannot become a wheel-rolling
king, and, fifth, she cannot become a buddha.[6] Indeed, even the
Buddha himself felt pity for the miserable state of woman!

"And as for the Three Duties: in her youth, a woman must obey
and serve her father; in her prime, she must obey and serve her
husband, and, in her old age, she must obey and serve her son.
Because of these strictures, it is taught, it is difficult for a woman to
enter buddhahood.[7]

"You mustn't waste energy on just anything. First, you must have compassion. Compassion lies in forgetting the self and being benevolent to others, rescuing them from danger, saving them from the brink of death, and showing sympathy to all. Second is humility, which lies in being wealthy yet never proud, in accumulating virtue through generous almsgiving, in paying obeisance to the heavens and treading lightly on the earth, and in never indulging in vain competition among friends. One who lives in this manner shows humility. Third is propriety. As the subject reveres his lord, so too the child obeys his parents. One must respect one's elders and be kind to one's juniors. The highly placed despise not their underlings, and the lowly seek not to disrupt the social order. Fourth is wisdom. To learn widely of the written word, to inquire into all manner of arts, to discard the old and embrace the new, always to examine everything twice and to revere the sages: this is wisdom. Fifth is sincerity: to speak honestly; if something is unrighteous, not to engage in it, if not virtuous, not to partake of it; to be earnest both inwardly and outwardly. This is sincerity.[8] You hate the brazier because you do not apprehend the truth of all this. Consider it well!

"That reminds me of a man named Teiran in old China who was so filial that he would remain awake attending to his parents throughout the night. After his mother died, he grieved at being parted from her. His despair led him to carve a wooden image of her and name it Mokuzō.[9] Day and night he paid his respects to it, offering freshly cut flowers and burning incense. Whenever anyone called for whatever reason, Teiran would consult it. Once a neighbor came by to borrow an axe. As usual, Teiran turned to the wooden figure to consult with it. Of course, being wood, it uttered not a word in response, but nonetheless Teiran refused to lend the axe. The neighbor was furious. Choosing a time when Teiran was out of the house, he stole in and split the image in two. Teiran returned, calling out, "Oh, Mokuzō, I'm home!" then spied the shattered image, blood spilling from it. He wept bitterly, wondering what could have happened. Soon he realized that his neighbor was the most likely culprit and came to blows with him. This dis-

ruption reached the ears of the Emperor, who punished the neighbor and awarded Teiran an office and stipend, according to the Book of Mōshu.[10]

"I was shocked to see blood pouring out from this brazier. You are old and frail; your life is more fleeting than the morning clouds, evening dew, or lamplight in the face of a gale. It's shameful for you to be so jealous of a brazier! You should abandon all attachments and devote yourself to prayer!" On and on he scolded her, waxing even more irate as he spoke.

The old woman heard him out, then said, "Yes, I understand what you've told me, and you're right. However, if the brazier were to let fly a spark in this tiny thatched hut, so small a shack that it fits only one straw mat—well, not only would the neighbors be down on our heads, but you and I would be in a terrible fix! We'd have nowhere to live! We keep two patchwork quilts to ward off the winter cold because it is written in *The Tale of Genji* and *The Book of Rites* that one blanket shall not serve to cover both man and woman.[11] It would be awful if the quilts were burned up! I have reason to hate that brazier!"

"You have a point," responded her husband. "You never know when fire or other disasters will occur. There have been fires in Kyoto, Sakai, and Kamakura, causing heavy losses to thousands of people, but there's no point bemoaning one's fate when something like that happens. Some men habitually succumb to avarice, invoking privilege to protect their own wives and family while plundering the property of others. Such people have no respect for anyone! Concerned only with their own livelihoods, they are unaware that they are draining others and causing untold harm. Men who boast of their own prosperity are usually disruptive and liable to sudden disaster. But why should I be hurt by calamity? I live here in this hut and keep to myself; poverty is my closest companion. I am ashamed of my years and neither venture out nor receive visitors. I derive my only comfort from gazing at the passing clouds and from my fervent anticipation of future salvation.

"Hear my words, dear granny! Those of deep sensitivity have always recited poetry and created linked verse. I too was drawn to

the path of poetry in my younger days. Don't you know, granny, that each living creature, even the warbler nestling among the flowers and the frog living in the water, has its song to sing? And what's more, I've heard tell that poetry quells the hearts of demons and fierce warriors and eases relations between men and women.[12]

"As for the story of the warbler, once in a mountain temple there was an acolyte who passed away mysteriously. His master mourned long and bitterly. Then he listened carefully to a warbler who came every morning to sing in front of the temple. 'Sho yo mai cho rai fu so ken hon sei,' it sang.[13] He wrote down this odd song and saw that it created a poem:

Hatsu haru no	Each morning of early spring
ashita goto ni wa	I come hither, only to return
kitaredomo	to whence I came
awade zo kaeru	without encountering you.
moto no sumika ni	

The bird's expression was truly marvelous.

"Now, as for the frog's poem, in the tracks of a frog creeping along a beach at Sumiyoshi was clearly revealed a poem that read:

Sumiyoshi no	He who has seen and not forgotten
hama wa mirume shi	the sea grasses of Sumiyoshi shore
wasurezu wa	shall again see his beloved
kari ni mo hito ni	if for but a moment.
mata towarenuru	

This also signified something to the beholder, and the poem became well known to all.[14]

"Now, as for softening the hearts of demons and fierce warriors: long ago at a place called Suzuka Mountain, on the border of Ise and Owari provinces, lived a group of obstreperous barbarians named Chikata, who caused great harm to numbers of people. General Tamura no Sakanoue was sent to quell them. He brought all the force of his military prowess to bear on them, but a crowd of demons with supernatural powers fended him off, and his attack was unsuccessful. At last, when it appeared that they would never submit, he recited:

> Tsuchi mo ki mo   The earth and the trees too—
> waga okimi no   all are my lord's domain;
> kuni nareba   where could there be
> izuku ka oni no   a haven for demons?
> sumika naran

Thus, he ordered them to depart, using poetic phrasing.[15] In this way, people have come to value poetry.

"What's more, the path of poetry also softens relations between men and women and brings comfort to the hearts of fierce warriors. It is wrong to despise the path: whether one is highly placed or humble, poetry is an expedient means to teach us of the passage of youth into old age and a guide to the way of religious devotion. Its value must never be taken lightly!

"The Bodhidharma manifested himself in human form and met Prince Shotoku on Mount Kataoka. When he saw the Bodhidharma prostrate on the side of the mountain, the prince recited:

> Shinateru ya   Oh traveler!
> Kataoka yama no   You must know sadness,
> ii ni uete   lying starved for sustenance
> fuseru tabibito   on shining sloped Kataoka.
> aware o ya shiru

It is said that the Bodhidharma's response was delivered in verse as well.[16] The saints Saichō, Kōbō Daishi, Engaku, and Gyōgi all composed poetry.

"In the reign of Emperor Heijō, the *Manyo'shū* poetry anthology was compiled; in the reign of Daigo, the *Kokinshū;* in the reign of Murakami, the *Gosenshū;* in the reign of Kazan, the *Shūishū;* and in the same era, the *Kin'yōshū.* In the reign of Emperor Shūtoku, the *Shikashū* was compiled; in the reign of Go

Toba, the *Shinkokinshū;* in the reign of Kameyama, the *Shokuko-kinshū;* and in the same era, the *Shoku Gosenshū* was compiled.[17]

"Then there are the verses of the collection called *A Hundred Poets' Hundred Poems,*[18] which Lord Teika copied down at his villa at Ogura. Since the poetry submitted for the *Shinkokinshū* anthology had all been composed by flawless persons, Teika found it difficult to judge among them and so included them all in that collection. But it distressed him that some poems, although beautiful, lacked quality, so he selected only a hundred of the most superior, wrote them down on screens and paperboards, and gazed at them morning and night. After his death, this collection was called *A Hundred Poets' Hundred Poems* by imperial decree. The Emperor and his followers treasured the Path of Poetry, and all in the realm revere it. I find it deplorable that you do not but rather obstinately persist in your jealousy of this brazier!

"Lord Shunzei wrote poetry in the dead of night under the faltering lamplight, a battered court hat pulled low over his ears, an old quilt drawn around his shoulders, tears running down his face as he pondered. He called his collection of poems *The Paulownia Brazier.*[19] When complimented on the excellence of his verse, Shunzei refused all praise, protesting that he himself was but a paulownia brazier. The Path of Poetry has achieved great heights through such efforts, and one should never deride it on any account.

"Once a certain man was asked to compose a poem incorporating the terms *twisted wisteria* and *paulownia brazier* along with his own name, Yorimasa. He composed:

Se wa hitari	Flood rapids spill
maki no fuchiochi	over the depths of Makino,
tamari mizu	pools of water spreading
Hiokesaika ni	as far as Hiokesaika.[20]
yorimazaruran	

In this way, he was able to use *paulownia brazier* in a difficult poetic task.

"Then there is the poem by Izumi Shikibu:

Anakashiko	Of your sooty bottom
hito ni kataru na	concealed in ashes
kiribioke	don't tell a soul,
mata uchikakuru	wooden brazier.[21]
soko no arisama	

"Now, this old man may not be able to match poetry like that, but nevertheless I feel compelled to compose these lines:

Atatamuru	Traces of warmth
ato no ubagoze	left by dear granny—
hi ni usuku	thin rays of dawn alight
naru akatsuki wa	on scattered silken sleeves."
kinuginu no sode	

Then the old woman spoke up. "I've suffered beating, scolding, shame, and lectures on poetry, all on account of that brazier. How mortifying this is! But jealousy too has been around for a long, long time as well. It's even in *The Tale of Genji,* where the carriage dispute at the Kamo festival led Lady Rokujō to harbor such a bitter jealousy of Lady Aoi that she turned into a demon and killed her rival.[22]

"*The Tales of the Heike* tell of a lady who wanted to kill her husband's new wife. She journeyed to the Kibune Myōjin shrine and feverishly petitioned the god to transform her into a demon so that she could destroy her rival and all the rival's relations, sparing not a soul. One night the god appeared to her in a dream and told her that she must first alter her appearance, then immerse herself in the waters of the Uji River for twenty-one days. If she followed these instructions, her petition would be granted. The woman was overjoyed. On her return from the shrine, she stopped in a deserted area and parted her hair in five bunches, fashioning them into horns. She painted her face vermillion, applied cinnabar to her body, and placed an iron ring on her head. She then ignited two pine torches and clamped them between her teeth. Late at night, when all was still, she went out into the road and headed south to Uji. Five flames shot up from her head, and all who saw her were so frightened that they fainted dead away.

"When she arrived at the Uji rapids, she immersed herself for twenty-one days. Just as the god had promised, she was transformed into a demon. She is called the Lady of the Uji Bridge. As a demon, she put an end not only to her rival but also to the husband who had cast her aside and all his family, without regard for rank or gender.[23]

"There once was a demon who took the form of a beautiful woman in order to ensnare men. It so terrorized the capital that everyone kept their gates firmly shut, remaining inside and admitting no one, even in broad daylight. Tsuna, Kintoki, Sadamitsu, and Suetaka, retainers of Yorimitsu, were known as the Four Guardian Kings of Raikō.[24] Tsuna was born in a village called Hishida in Musashi Province and therefore was called Hishida Genji.

"Yorimitsu once sent Tsuna on an errand to the corner of First Avenue and Ōmiya. It was late at night, and the wary Tsuna had brought his sword, Beardcutter. His mission accomplished, he was crossing the bridge at First and Horikawa when he caught sight of a young woman of no more than twenty standing at the edge of the river. She was incomparably beautiful, with skin as white as snow. She wore a white silk robe lined in red, carried a sutra scroll in one hand, and was heading south quite alone, unaccompanied by any servants. 'Where are you going?' she asked. 'I am a lone woman with no escort on my way down to Fifth Avenue. It's so dark and frightening out here; won't you please take me?' she appealed.

"She looked gratified when Tsuna consented. He drew up beside her and helped her mount. Taking his place behind her, he headed south down the east side of the river. They had no sooner entered a short way down Masaji Lane than the lady turned back and said, 'I have no business in Fifth Avenue. I live outside the capital. Please take me there.'

" 'I'll take you wherever you'd like,' replied Tsuna.

"Suddenly her ravishing beauty changed to the fearsome countenance of a demon. 'I'm going to that mountain!' it screamed. Turning around and grabbing Tsuna by the topknot, it flew off northwest toward Mount Atago.[25]

"Tsuna had been prepared for this. Without blinking an eye, he unsheathed his sword Beardcutter and lopped off the demon's hand. Tsuna toppled down on the roof of Kitano Shrine, and the demon flew off to the mountain, even though its hand had been severed. How frightening! So it's written in *The Tales of the Heike*.[26]

"Yes, there have been some pretty vengeful women! You shouldn't make light of my complaint. Do you think it's been easy being married to you and living in this miserable shack? My parents lived in the capital as servants to gentlefolk who spent their time amusing themselves with poetry and music and passed each day composing verse on the blossom-filled spring and the maple-tinged autumn. A bit of it has remained with me to this day.

"It is written in *The Tales of Ise* that Narihira fell so desperately in love with a woman that he was unable to repress his passion. Cutting off the hem of a shinobu-grass-patterned hunting robe, he wrote on it:

Kasuga no	My heart is in wild disarray
wakamurasaki no	that knows no bounds—
surigoromo	like this robe, printed in the
shinobu no midare	hidden grasses of Kasuga field.
kagiri shirarezu	

The lady was impressed with this verse. In return, she recited Kawara no Sadaijin's verse:

Michinoku no	Who could have caused
shinobu mojizuri	this wild disarray
dare yue ni	like grass patterns of Michinoku?
midare somenishi	Surely not myself!
ware naranaku ni	

People of old were so admirably elegant![27]

"That reminds me of an old poem from *The Tale of Genji* that goes like this:

Ubasoku ga	Our pious guide
okonau michi o	will lead us on the path
shirube ni koso	of the world to come,
komu yo mo fukaki	and our vows will be ever deep.[28]
chigiri taezu na	

I don't know the real significance of this, but it seems to mean that you should cleave to me and never allow your feelings to change, both in this life and in the one to come. Thus, our bond will grow so strong that we will share the same lotus leaf, united in prayer.

"And now please forgive my sin of breaking the brazier," she pleaded.

The old man nodded vigorously in assent. "You have spoken impressively. Indeed, a woman's worth is not to be measured by her looks or figure. I hadn't realized that you were capable of such a genteel response. Everything occurs within a dream—a dream of lightning flashes and morning dew. Life is so fleeting! We must cast off everything and look to the next world, regarding that brazier as none other than a friendly guide to hasten us on our way to salvation."

NOTES

1. This parodies a theme appearing in a number of early sources and later variations. Any one of the poems using the metaphor for loneliness expressed in the image of the single-sleeved robe may have served as the inspiration for the parody. One of the more likely candidates is *Kokinshū* no. 689: "Again tonight does she spread / a lone sleeve on a narrow mat? / The Lady of Uji Bridge / surely waits for me."

2. *Ichigan no kame ni hōrai*, perhaps a humorous mixed metaphor derived from an aphorism referring to the unlikely and felicitous circumstance of a blind (or one-eyed) turtle surfacing the water and entering a hole in a piece of driftwood *(ichigan no kame fuboku ni au)*; a lucky shot in the dark. Mount Hōrai is a mythical peak in the eastern seas.

3. A reference to Yu Tzu and Bai Yang, a couple who were so devoted to each other that after their death they became birds in order to remain together forever.

4. "I can fend for myself" is at best an approximation of an exceedingly cryptic line—"na wa hiro koso irubekere, hakarau shisai ari"—which might also be rendered, "I am well known and have the means to get by."

5. The Buddha, the Law, and the Buddhist Community.

6. I have followed Leon Hurvitz's translation in *Scripture of the Lotus Blossom of the Fine Dharma* (New York: Columbia University Press, 1976), p. 201.

7. The Three Duties of Women are of Confucian origin but were incorporated into Buddhist thought in China and Japan. The Five Hindrances and the Three Duties were often invoked in support of the inferiority of women. A similar reference appears in *Lazy Tarō*.

8. The old man has listed the Five Virtuous Conducts of Confucianism.

9. Lit., "wooden image," but used here as a name.

10. The text (or the old man) mistakenly attributes this tale of filial piety to the *Book of Mencius*. This may be a miscopying of *Mo gyū*, a collection of Chinese admonitory tales, but the story is not to be found there either. It was assimilated into Japanese lore quite early and also appears in the otogi-zōshi *Nijūshiko*. Old Lady Tokiwa refers to it when she berates her children.

11. To my knowledge, no such passage occurs in either work.

12. This closely follows the Japanese preface to the *Kokinshū*.

13. The bird's song is written in Chinese characters. Read in Japanese, with poetic diction added, it becomes the poem cited.

14. The stories of the bird and the frog appear together in several medieval sources. They seem to be most directly related to, and are probably derived from, medieval commentaries on the *Kokinshū*.

15. The text has presented a slightly altered version of the legend than that of other early sources, which state that a nobleman named Fujiwara no Chikata, rather than a group of barbarians named Chikata, led the uprising against the Emperor.

16. This legend appears in a number of sources, among them the *Nihon shoki*, the *Nihon ryōiki*, the *Konjaku monogatari*, and the *Shasekishū*.

17. Of this long list of imperial poetry anthologies, only the dating of the *Kin'yōshū* is incorrect; it was compiled in the reign of Emperor Shirakawa.

18. *Hyakunin isshū*.

19. *The Pawlonia Brazier (Kiribioke)* is actually a collection of poetic dicta attributed to Teika, in which he reports this anecdote about his father Shunzei.

20. Minamoto no Yorimasa (1104–1180) was a warrior and accomplished poet active in the Genpei wars. This poetic feat, accomplished through puns and clever parsing, does not translate well. The anecdote appears in a variant text of the *Tales of the Heike,* the *Heike monogatari Nagato bon.*

21. There is no evidence that the famed poetess Izumi Shikibu ever composed this poem.

22. Recounted in chap. 9, "Aoi," of *The Tale of Genji.*

23. This tale of jealousy and revenge, also recounted in the otogi-zōshi and nō play, both titled *Kanawa,* appears in another variant of *The Tales of the Heike,* the *Yashiro bon Heike monogatari.*

24. *Raikō shitenno.* In Buddhism, the Four Guardian Kings guard each of the four compass points. The phrase was used to describe the most trusted retainers of a lord, in this case, Minamoto no Yorimitsu, also called Raikō.

25. Mount Atago has traditionally been thought of as an abode of demons.

26. It is not clear how the Tsuna story exemplifies the theme of jealousy. Rather, it reveals the potential demon in every woman. The tale is included in close proximity to that of the Lady of Uji Bridge in the *Yashiro bon Heike monogatari.*

27. The text has correctly cited the poems in the first episode of *The Tales of Ise* but has changed the context. The latter poem was originally described as having served as the inspiration for, rather than the response to, Narihira's poem.

28. This is a slight misquotation of a poem appearing in chap. 4, "Yugao," of *The Tale of Genji.*

The Little Man

Ko otoko no sōshi

The theme of a dwarf whose poetic talents enable him to win the hand of a beautiful woman and worldly riches must have been extremely popular among medieval Japanese audiences, to judge from the number and variety of extant manuscripts that tell the same basic story. *The Little Man* is rooted in ancient legends, folktales of upward mobility, Buddhist-influenced accounts of the tribulations of deities, and the marriage quest *(tsuma goi)* tale tradition. The tiny hero with hidden dynamic power may be traced to legendary figures associated with the thundergod, and it is no wonder that, in almost all stories in which he appears, ultimately he is revealed to be a god. The concluding lines, "Those who read this book will thereby invoke the sacred names of the gods," indicate that the physical text had a talismanic function derived from sacred associations.

The complex of some eleven tales featuring a gifted dwarf may be divided into three strains: the *Ko otoko* (Little man) line, to which belongs *The Little Man* translated here; the *Issun bōshi* (Little one-inch) line, most familiar to modern readers through its folktale variants; and the *Hikyūdono* (Lord dwarf) line, an intermediate version containing elements from the other two. As the reader will notice, *Lazy Tarō* shares the same basic plot as well as several specific features, including a humorous scene replete with witty poem. While the paucity of information relating to otogi-zōshi renders it difficult to trace precise paths of textual influence and descent, most scholars agree that the Ko otoko line is the prototype that spawned the other related texts.

This translation is based on the text printed without annotations in *Muromachi jidai monogatari taisei* (3:595–605), transcribed from a scroll in the collection of the Akagi bunko. This scroll is profusely illustrated, containing eighteen scenes replete with captions, described here in the notes. It was selected for translation for its unusual length and detail among the several Ko otoko tales.[1] The illustrations reproduced here, from another Ko otoko variant in scroll form dated to the late Muromachi period, have been provided through the courtesy of the Tenri Library.

Long ago in the Kuromoto District of Yamashiro Province[2] there lived a little man only one foot tall and nine inches[3] in breadth. Thought he to himself, "There's nothing at all I can do hidden away like this in the country. If only I could go to the capital and serve under someone; then I might be awarded a province or district to govern!" And so quite abruptly he took off alone for the capital.

On his arrival, he paused at an intersection of two sidestreets. He intended to call on someone and announce himself, but wondered about his approach. If he spoke out loudly, people might laugh at the incongruity between his great voice and his tiny size; then again, if he spoke softly, they might think him an inconsequential child. After some anxious vacillation, he finally made up his mind and raised his voice in a booming shout. A woman[4] emerged from a house to find out who had called, looked, but saw no one. Then something rustled beneath a clump of grasses off to the side; she peered down and realized that it was human. "Oh, how adorable! He's so cute! So this is what a little man looks like!" she cried. A group of townsmen gathered round to stare at him.

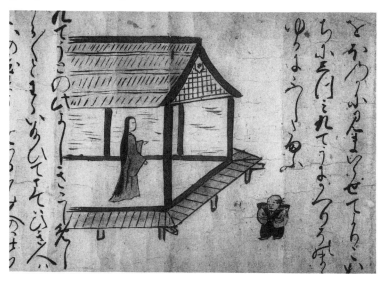

"It must be karma from some previous life," he thought, "to be this small, yet a human being like everyone else." In his despair he composed a verse:

Saki no yo ni   What sin did I commit
ikanaru tsumi no   in a former life—
mukai ka ya   to be born to this body
shaku ni mo taranu   barely a foot tall?
mi to mumareken

Sick at heart, he stood rooted to the spot, ashamed and humiliated.[5]

Nothing had come of this venture, so he went elsewhere and announced himself. The lady of the house emerged in response and looked around, but saw no one. "Odd," she thought, glancing here and there, then finally spotted something hidden in some sparsely growing grasses. "How strange! Are you a man?" she inquired.

"Yes, I am," he responded.

"Where did you come from?"

"I am from Kuromoto District, where I am called the Provisional Governor.[6] I was curious about the capital, so I came here to see if I could find service as a retainer to someone," he explained.

"Then stay here. Perhaps I can use you for amusement.[7] If you would like to perform some service for me, you may rake up the pine needles on Kiyomizu Mountain once a day."

The little man was mortified that she considered him so mean and insignificant that she would have him perform drudgery like this. Service at the palace, where they would have him carry out duties of substance, might lead to the grant of a province or village, and his whole family would flourish. Nonetheless, he performed his duties as instructed. Every day he went to Kiyomizu, where he would worship at the temple and sweep up the pine needles on the mountainside, the sounds of the waterfall and whistling winds filling him with sadness. "I amount to no more than the shadow of the twigs on this rake," he reflected forlornly.[8]

Once he became weary and lay down to take a nap; when he raised his head, he saw throngs of people crossing the Todorogi Bridge[9] on their return from worship, for it was the festival of the eighteenth of the month.[10] Among them was an aristocratic lady, so beautiful that he gazed at her entranced. Yōhiki[11] of old or even the angels above could not compare with her. She wore sixteen-layer robes of green lined with red plum, and the figure she cut was too exquisite for words. She was accompanied by various attendants.

It took but one glance to throw the little man's heart into turmoil. As a morning glory withered in the blaze of the noonday sun or a torch wick extinguished by hurricane winds, he completely lost his grip on reality; his very existence was more ephemeral than morning dew on a blade of grass.[12]

Gradually the little man revived, calmed himself, and arose. He removed the bundle of needles from his back and tossed them aside, then stealthily followed after her to see where she lived. He watched her enter the gate of a residence next to the mountain and peeked inside. He was small enough to hide under the grasses, so no one realized that he was there.[13]

When he returned to the hill where he had been working, he was dismayed to see that all his pine needles had been stolen. He reflected bitterly on his sad lot in life. Someone of his stature hardly counted as a person at all, he thought in despair. Raking together some more needles, he hoisted them on his back and returned home to his mistress.[14]

From that day on, the little man was sunken prostrate in a daze, his very being as insubstantial as a dewdrop:

Waga koi wa	Like a rock in the offing,
shioi ni mienu	unseen even in low tides,
oki no ishi	unknown to all, washed by
hito koso shirane	waves of tears, is my love.
kawaku ma mo nashi	

He wanted to share his anguish with someone but could do naught but recite:

Morotomo ni	If only there were
aware to omou	a sympathetic companion
hito mogana	to whom I could relate
tsutsumu koishiki	my hidden love and grief!
uki o kataran	

Thus he languished without telling a soul. Even so, his mistress heard his lamentations and was moved by pity to send a serving lady named Suodono to ascertain the cause of his distress. Although the little man had not intended to tell anyone of his problems, he was unable to suppress his emotion in the face of these inquiries. He poured out everything that had happened, from beginning to end. Suodono listened to his story and, unbelievable though it seemed, reported it all back to the lady of the house.

"It is indeed touching," said her mistress. "From past through present, there has always been this feeling called love, which softens men's hearts and fills them with deep emotion. Such is the way of this sad world that love persists from the present life to the next. We must comfort him."

Suodono returned to the little man and instructed him to write out everything he felt; she would deliver the message to his beloved. Transported with happiness, he hurriedly arose. With a brush made of wood from Asaka Mountain and jet-black ink, he wrote out his declaration of love on a thin sheet of paper:

Kimi sama wa	Thou art a cherry blossom
matsu no ha yama no	hidden by a veil of mist
michishiba no	enwreathing the grasses
kasumi no shita no	by the wayfarer
sakurabana	waiting at Evergreen Mountain.
watatsu umi no	Do clouds cut across the moon
yokogiru kumo no	shining on broad seas?
murasaki no nezuri	Deep hues of lavender longing,
katawara ni uchiyosuru	drenched in waves constantly
nami no hiru wo	thundering against the shore.[15]
da ni matanu ka na	

He folded it in the Yamato style, secured it with a spray of pine needles, and gave it to Suodono.[16]

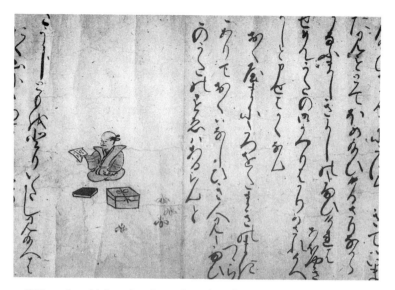

"How should I reply when she asks where the letter is from and who sent it?" asked Suodono.

"Say that it is from the Provisional Governor, Steward of Kuromoto District, Yamashiro Province," he responded.

Suodono listened carefully and delivered it as instructed. Though the lady knew not who it was from, she was bound to accept it graciously, be the sender high or humble.[17] Well known in the capital as a great beauty, the lady constantly received numerous addresses from aristocrats and those privy to the imperial family itself. Yet, among this barrage of letters, never had she received a more beautiful, impressively penned, or elegantly expressed missive than the present one.

"Waiting at Evergreen Mountain means that he will wait for me forever," she interpreted, "the clouds cutting across the moon that he wonders if there is another man, the deep hues of lavender that he is deeply in love with me,[18] and the waves thundering against the shore, that his sleeves are always wet with tears." In response, she wrote:

Sora yuku kumo no   Some night in the future as distant
sue no yo ga   as the clouds floating in the skies . . .

Suodono returned and gave the little man her response. Filled with endless joy, he sat up energetically and studied it: it meant that he should visit nine days hence.[19] Waiting those nine days seemed nigh unto passing a thousand years.

Finally, on the appointed day, his mistress supplied him with clothing. He was bathed, then dressed in a tall hat and simple hunting costume. All these sartorial preparations were indeed amusing![20] He set out about ten in the morning, and it was not until six in the evening that he arrived at his destination, only three *chō*[21] distant.

The lady had prepared to receive him at the customary twilight trysting hour. Disappointed that her suitor failed to arrive, she was gazing disconsolately out in the garden when a tiny thing moving almost imperceptibly under a bush caught her attention. How strange! Could it be a supernatural being? She felt uneasy, but reasoned that, no matter what it was, the creature had a soul, and it must possess human feeling thus to employ the garden flowers as a token of its presence. And so she called out, "Whoever you are in there, please come out!"

Filled with joy, the little man recited in succession:

Shinobureba	Grown weak and pale
mi ni wa yasenikeri	from long suppression—
kurenai ni	would that my passion emerge
chishio no iro ni	in a crimson tide!
ikade ide namu	
Au to te mo	Though we shall meet tonight
ureshiku mo naki	I feel no joy
koyoi ka na	for dread of the dawn
asu no wakare o	and the parting it brings.
kanete omoeba	

With these expressions of love, the lady melted. She was touched by his refined sensibility, and her heart was deeply moved.[22]

The little man gazed up longingly. The veranda was higher than he was tall, and he was unable to scale it, so the lady obligingly took his hand and hoisted him up. Then she realized with mounting chagrin how small he was.[23]

"Must I be the lover of such a creature?" she thought, hastily shutting the sliding screen and disappearing inside. But the little man had no intention of giving up. He tapped on the screen, begging her for admittance, but she would not yield. Soon dawn began to break, and crows appeared. He recited:

Yo mo sugara	All through the night,
shoji yarido o	while I've tapped at your doors,
tataku ma ni	crows circled and cried
mine ni karasu no	around the high peaks.
naki wataru ka na	
Akuru ka to	Hoping in vain that it might open
tataku tsumado o	I've tapped at your little door—
ake mo se de	never expecting that dawn
kokoro no hoka ni	could have broken before you did.
yo koso akekere	

When the lady heard this, she realized that, even if he were a demon, his display of passion hardly merited dismissal. She shifted open the screen ever so slightly and called him in. The elated little man wondered what to do. If he opened it wide and entered boldly, she might think it unseemly of his own small stature;[24] if he opened it just slightly, she might think him a timid child. He made his decision and slid the screen wide open, only to break a koto that had been propped against it, rendering it totally useless. Since she had closed the screen from within, this was only to be expected:

Kami naranu	Alas, I am no god, and
waga mi no hodo zo	my stature a source of pain.
tsuraki ka na	The koto's smashed; my hopes are dashed—
kotowari nareba	I'm so abashed!
mono mo iwarezu[25]	

He was about to leave, but, on hearing his words, so touching and heartfelt, the lady had a change of heart and called him back in.[26]

Happy beyond belief, the little man entered her chamber and tearfully told her everything from the moment he had first seen her. The lady was filled with emotion, and her heart was extraordinarily moved. They lay down together, all reserve between them melting like ice by the shore as they dissolved into the deep pools of love. The little man was overjoyed.[27]

From that moment on they shared a profound love. In heaven they were as lovebirds, on earth branches of intertwined trees;[28] as deities they were as gods of union, as buddhas, gods of love. Indeed, their unchanging devotion, as eternal as verdant pines, was auspicious and wonderful beyond compare. Soon a child was born to them, followed shortly thereafter by another.

Although the little man's looks may have been less than comely, his wife cherished him nonetheless. They lived in abundance and flourished in everlasting love,[29] and they prospered as long as they lived. Their offspring thrived, and all lived long and healthy lives. Later, the little man appeared as the god of Gojō Shrine[30] and his wife as the Holy Kannon.[31] They fulfill the requests of all sentient beings and have vowed in particular to respond to the petitions of desperate lovers. Everyone should take care to worship them often.

One should always value oneself and learn an art. People with human compassion will always receive their due rewards. Those who read this book will thereby invoke the sacred names of these gods:

Kimi ga yo wa
chiyo no yachiyo o
sazareishi ni
iwao to narite
koke no musu made

May this august era
endure for thousands of years
until pebble turns to boulder
and moss grows upon it.[32]

Kimi ga yo no
hisashikarubeki
tameshi ni ya
kanete zo ueshi
Sumiyoshi no matsu

That this august era
may last ever long
the pines of Sumiyoshi
grow as a manifest token.

Nanigoto mo
kokoro ni kanau
onyo nareba
na o yukusue
sakae sakauru

One may attain his heart's desire
no matter what it may be.
Such is this reign:
may it shine and prosper forever.[33]

NOTES

1. In preparing the final revisions of this translation, I was assisted by Tokuda Kazuo's annotations to another Ko otoko variant contained in the newly published *Muromachi monogatari shū,* vol. 1.

2. Now part of present-day south Kyoto. Other texts state that he hails from the village of Yorima, Yamato District (present-day Nara Prefecture), and, in the Hikyūdono textual line, he is a native of the capital proper.

3. One *shaku;* eight *sun.*

4. The gender of this character is not specified in the text. I have made her female because a similar character in another text is female and because the verbal reaction is couched in feminine terms. Interestingly, the little man encounters few other men throughout the complex of dwarf stories.

5. The picture caption reads: "Please give lodgings to this out-of-towner! / My name is the Provisional Governor Toshihisa. / Oh, how tiny! How funny!"

6. *Gon no kami* translates as "provisional governor." His given name is Toshihisa. He may be assuming the title in order to impress people. Alternatively, the title may involve a pun, insofar as it is homophonous with "provisional god," a Shinto god manifested as an incarnation of a buddha or bodhisattva. According to the logic of syncretic Buddhism and the final outcome of this story, the little man is correct in asserting this to be his identity, although there is no textual clue that he is aware of his ultimate destiny.

7. The text reads *kyōjū no monoharai* (object of laughter throughout the city), a miscopying of *monowarai* (laughingstock). This incorporates a pun on *harai*, "sweep" or "rake."

8. The illustration depicts people laughing at him; the caption reads: "Hey, he's so small! / Aah, Hail Amida Buddha! What a sad world. / Look at him—he's so tiny! / He certainly is small! / Can this really be a person? / Well, well, is this a man or an insect? / Truly, it would be terrible to marry a man like that. / Awful, isn't it?"

9. A bridge leading to the temple complex.

10. The eighteenth of every month was a festival day at Kiyomizu.

11. Yang Kuei Fei, the legendary Chinese beauty described in "The Song of Unending Sorrow."

12. The picture caption reads: "What do you suppose that is?"

13. The picture caption reads: "Did he say something? / Oh, how funny! / As much as you try to deny it, you can't: he's right here. Isn't it great?"

14. The picture caption reads: "What anguish! That such an insignificant person as I should be in love like this! What anguish! I'm so miserable!" This verse expresses his sadness: "Yoshi wakare / akade da ni mo ya / hazubeki ni / to wa omoedo / nururu sode ka na" (So soon parted / though not yet fulfilled / though I should be ashamed of myself / my sleeves are yet wet with tears).

15. This rambling and ornate billet-doux consists of a series of poetic riddles. Such communications demonstrate a suitor's poetic wit and are common in literary depictions of medieval courtship.

16. The picture caption reads: "I hope that she understands my message. My very life hangs on it. / I'll deliver your letter without fail (Suodono)."

17. Contemporary wisdom had it that showing kindess to others inevitably brought good fortune to oneself.

18. Lavender was the color of affinity.

19. It is unclear how the message can be interpreted in this way.

20. The picture caption reads: "Truly! / Just look at him in those robes! / Wear this. (Suodono) / He looks good in the hat and robe. / How could one ignore good looks like this?"

21. One chō is equal to approximately 109 meters.

22. The picture caption reads: "Come here! / How wonderful to be praised! No one is happier than Toshihisa." I have omitted an undecipherable phrase, *kashimi to te,* from the beginning.

23. The picture caption reads: "Do not be alarmed! I am not a suspicious creature!"

24. *Mi no hodo* is translated as "stature" in an attempt to approximate the Japanese term, which incorporates both physical size and social standing.

25. The last two lines of this poem also appear at the end of *Lazy Tarō,* where they employ the same pun on *kotowari,* "to break a koto" and "truth" or "reason." In most other Ko otoko texts, the poem begins with *Kazu naranu* (insignificant; counting for nothing) rather than *kami naranu* (no god am I).

26. The poem is followed by an illustration of the woman calling the little man back. The caption reads: "It is said that women are deeply sinful, but a woman with this kind of sensibility is sure to go to paradise."

27. The picture caption reads: "This must be an inevitable bond from a former life."

28. These lines appear at the end of "The Song of Unending Sorrow."

29. An illustration of the little man's household is captioned: "Come here, children! (nurse) / They certainly are fine children! If they're as talented as their father, no one will ever be able to laugh at them."

30. One of the two tutelary gods of the Gojō Tenjin shrine in Kyoto is Sukunabiko no omikoto, said to have been a tiny god, to which the little man may be traced.

31. Shōkannon, the most common of the six manifestations of the Kannon.

32. The Japanese believed that pebbles grew to boulders over the ages.

33. The last three poems, appended only to this particular Ko otoko text, convey typical expressions of felicity, of which poetic variations abound.

The Tale of Dōjōji

Dōjōji monogatari

This otogi-zōshi *Tale of Dōjōji* is but one of many variations on the famous Dōjōji legend to appear throughout Japanese literary and folk tradition. To this day, the monk Anchin and his lust-driven female pursuer are synonymous with destructive passion in the mind of every modern Japanese. Narrative versions of the legend appear in a number of tale collections, including the twelfth-century *Konjaku monogatari shū,* the *Hokekyōkenki,* the Edo period *Ugetsu monogatari* by Ueda Akinari, and countless modern folktale collections and retellings.[1] Both the nō and the *kabuki* theaters contain in their repertoires dramatic explorations of the theme, and the priests of Dōjōji Temple still offer tourists and pilgrims oral recitations of their version, adjusted to suit the taste of modern audiences, of the handscroll in their possession.

The legend of Dōjōji was originally based on ancient rain-invoking rituals; later misogynist tendencies in ascetic Buddhism gave rise to the association with female lust and desire. Dragons and serpents have long been associated with bodies of water and rain clouds and are invoked in rain-making rituals. In some temple rituals still performed today, a bell is lowered into a body of water, and the gratified serpent god causes rain to fall; in others, priests perform an exorcism of an effigy of a serpent wrapped around a temple bell, again in order to bring rain. Serpents are also associated with the baser emotions of lust and rage, and folklore contains numerous examples of women transformed into serpentine creatures by hatred, desire, or jealousy, as seen in the ending to *The King of Farts.*

There exist several otogi-zōshi versions of the Dōjōji tale; this is the longest and most detailed I have encountered. A fascinating amalgamation of several genres, among them poetry and poetic commentary, the travelogue, the sermon, the nō libretto, the tale of origins *(engi),* and the setsuwa, it is an excellent example of the tendency in otogi-zōshi to synthesize bits and pieces of contemporary culture into a narrative whole. The narrative shifts from genre to genre: the terse, stark, sermon-like enumeration of examples of lust in the human and natural world gives way to a highly lyrical, densely poetic prose in the initial travel section. This in turn is replaced by solemn sermons, then a travelogue recounting origins and anecdotes about the places through which Anchin passes. Anchin's is the standard route taken by Kumano-bound pilgrims from the Kyoto area; all the place names and associations mentioned would have been familiar to the audience from personal experience or hearsay. The tale of the origins of the Kumano shrine complex is derived from local legends that almost every Kumano pilgrim would have heard. Parts of the final exorcism appear to have been borrowed directly from the nō libretto, other parts from Buddhist lore. The concluding homily is an explication of and paean to the highly popular Lotus Sutra. I have kept notes to an absolute minimum; full annotation would require far more space than appropriate to a collection of this nature.

This translation is based on the illustrated printed booklet set dated 1660 in the collection of the Keio University Library, transcribed without annotations in *Muromachi jidai monogatari taisei* (4:104–124). The illustrations are from the same set and have been provided through the courtesy of the Keio University Library. At the end of the manuscript is a colophonic inscription with the name of the printer, one Hishiya Seibeiei, his address in Kyoto (Tomonikōji nijō agaru ni chōme), and the date, the twelfth month of 1660 (Manji 3).

Part 1

Nothing is more fearsome than the ways of sexual desire. Horses in spring mate with passionate ferocity; insects of summer flame with lust. Even a mighty elephant may be bound fast by a rope fashioned from a woman's hair, and the deer of autumn are drawn by the notes issuing from a flute made of clogs once worn by a woman.² The hermit named "One Horn," whose powers were great enough to capture and confine within a cave the rain dragons of all the seas, lost his magical abilities when he succumbed to a beautiful woman named Senda;³ the holy priest of Shiga, a saint with a firm determination to attain Buddhahood, fell to the Lady of Kyōgoku and lost his good name in the flow of love pledges.⁴ The dharma emperor Kazan rejected his lofty throne and took holy vows, only to fall to a serving woman named Nakatsukasa. Among the myriad examples of men who have lost the world and thrown away their lives because of a woman is one account of a most terrifyingly strong attachment.

At the Kurama Temple, in the Otagi District of Yamashiro Province, lived a monk named Anchin who maintained a strong desire for salvation and a steadfast belief in the power of the Kumano deities. One day, he suddenly made up his mind to undertake the arduous pilgrimage to Kumano.⁵ Leaving the door to his dear familiar hut open to greet the dawn, he departed like the wisp of smoke rising from the lamp left hanging on the wall.

Morning light played over his ink-black sleeves and the pale cherry blossoms growing on dark Kurama Mountain. As pining winds from the peak lifted the morning mists from the foothills, the now distant temple eaves were but faintly visible. Pressing on, he passed the foot of the mountain; on the plain, new foliage blanketed with dew reflected the lingering moon at Mizoro Pond. He paused to worship at the shrine of Tadasu, whose gods examine the lies in a person's heart. Looking back, he could see the sacred grounds of the buddhas and bodhisattvas, established by Saichō on cloud-wreathed Mount Hiei. Far off to his left, a white mantle of wild cherry mingled with crimson azalea, weaving a patterned brocade on the mountainside. Though the spring hues of Yoshida were lovely, and Gion, Kiyomizu, and Washinoyama in the eastern hills serene, the bell of Chōraku Temple resounded profoundly beyond all the blossoms. Passing through the village of Yasaka, his eye was caught by the funeral pyres of Toribe cremation grounds, and he mused on the foolish souls of men who, even as they watch the smoke rising, think that such a fate befalls only others—never themselves.

This sad capricious world is even more fleeting than dew on a leaf or foam on the waters, than bonfires in the night or a brief flash of lightning. In the morning of life, one is bright and beautiful; by evening, naught but a dry skeleton in a field, the memorial effigy moldering and the grave name indistinguishable. Akinori once wrote of this in a poem:

Nobe mireba	Looking at the fields,
mukashi no hito ya	I wonder who they were—
tare naramu	those men of old under the moss,
sono na mo shiranu	their names forgotten.[6]
koke no shita ka na	

The evanescence of life could be likened to the parable of a man who ventures far off on a plain. Suddenly he is pursued by a tiger who tries to devour him, so he runs into a deep well-like cavern. Grasping onto some weeds growing halfway down, he looks below, where he sees a poisonous serpent, red tongue slicking to and fro in its gaping mouth, waiting to eat him should he fall. He looks up again, only to see the tiger, its jaws open wide, waiting to eat him should he ascend. Then two rats, one black and one white, nibble in turn at the weed's roots. The terrified man realizes that the roots will give way at any moment. Just then, droplets from a tree overhead fall into his mouth. They are as sweet as nectar, and he becomes so attached to them that he forgets all his troubles.

The tiger is sinful karma clinging to us all; the bottom of the well, hell itself. The weeds are the energy of life; the two rats, the passage of time. The serpent is the demon guardian of hell; the sweet nectar, the five desires of the flesh. Sentient beings—those of grievous and petty sins alike—are unaware that death, the avatar of impermanence, pursues them night and day and that the never-ending constriction of their flesh proceeds from the roots of these weeds. How lamentable!

Life does not long endure; at any moment one may tumble into the evil realm of hell. All must recognize that they are ready prey to the guardian demons of hell. Just as the nectar from the tree exudes sweetness, so too do the six senses quiver when stimulated. The eyes see color, arousing desire; the ears hear sound, awakening attachment; the nose smells fragrance, sending the heart astray; the tongue savors all kinds of flavors, finding some sweet and some bitter; the flesh senses touch, kindling sensual desire; the heart feels a multitude of emotions and is moved to joy, anger, pity, or sorrow. Forgetting about the eternal suffering to come, mistaking the impermanent for the everlasting, men drown in the desires awakened by these six senses. Though they witness flowers scatter and leaves fall, they remain oblivious to the truth of impermanence as they fret from dawn to dusk over the petty affairs of this sad world, never giving thought to the afterlife.

The flesh has its sins of killing, stealing, and adultery, the mouth its sins of lying, idle chatter, and fomenting discord, and the heart its sins of greed, anger, and stupidity. Drawn into the net of such evil passions, men turn from darkness further into darkness, ever deaf to the teaching of the Buddha. This sad world will not endure forever. Izumi Shikibu expressed this in a verse sent to Priest Shokku:

Kuraki yori	Now must I venture
kuraki michi ni zo	from darkness to a darker way.
irinu beki	May the moon at the mountain rim
haruka ni terase	shine clearly on my path.[7]
yama no ha no tsuki	

One may seal himself within an iron castle or a hard rock, but death may not be evaded. This is evident from the parable of the

four wizards who desired to prolong their lives. These wizards used their magical powers to create an elixir of longevity, but, since everything is impermanent, soon even they reached the end of their years. Their powers of foresight told them that they had but seven days to live. Together they lamented, each trying to think of a place where death would be unable to reach him. One, declaring that no one could find him if he ascended to the sky and dwelt among the clouds, flew up to the heavens to hide. Another, saying that death could not reach him within the waves of the deep, dove into the ocean and hid. The third, saying that not even an emissary from the King of Hell could find him among the crowds of a city, concealed himself there. The fourth, stating that no manner of death could come to him if he broke open a mountain and leaped within, went to dwell inside a mountain. After the seven days had passed, each and every one of the four wizards died. Even these sages with their magical powers were unable to evade the pain of death. Priest Tōren wrote of this:

Sari tomo to	Though death was unavoidable,
yae no shioji ni	I entered the long sea ways,
irishikado	yet there too
soko ni mo oi no	the waves of age engulfed me.[8]
nami wa tachikeri	

As he passed by the crowds at the eastern temple, Tōji, Anchin wondered where his journey would end. Scanning the distant horizon, he could see the lovers' graves of Toba, and Autumn Hill. Shadows playing on the water coursing down the Amida Rapids brought to mind the vessel of the Universal Vow. Now far removed from the moon-bathed capital, he arrived at the Yodo River crossing. As the ferry crossed the face of the waters, droplets from the poles wet his sleeves, drenching his traveling robes. He passed the village of Kinya and the old imperial hunting grounds, where pheasants cried in the Katano fields. Gnarled branches of cherry blossoms drooped along the shoreline, but of Prince Koretaka and his evening diversions there remained naught but a dim memory.[9]

He pushed on further, passing Treasure Temple[10] with its image of the Thousand-Armed Kannon, where votive lights cast deep shadows, and through Niwatori village, where fowl gave tidings of dawn. The glint of the brilliant morning sun was reflected in the jewel-like glitter of dew on a flower. He passed by the village of Kōri and soon arrived at Eguchi. Here it was that long ago the monk Saigyō, stranded by rain and dark while undertaking a pilgrimage, requested shelter. When the request was denied, he recited:

Yo no naka o	'Tis painful enough
itou made koso	to have rejected the world,
katakarame	yet now you begrudge me
kari no yadori o	a brief night's lodging.[11]
oshimu kimi ka na	

Anchin pushed on, unbidden murmurs from the night waves at Kanzakiya filling his ears. Just past Watanabe, he arrived at the Temple of the Heavenly Kings.[12]

This temple, built by Prince Shotoku of the Sui Tennō clan, derived its name from the images of the Four Heavenly Kings sheltered there.[13] Prince Shotoku was a manifestation of the Savior Kannon, who assumed the form of the prince in order to save all sentient beings. A golden figure once appeared in a dream to the consort of the emperor Yōmei,[14] announcing that he was a buddha of salvation and would take shelter within her womb. No sooner had he spoken than he leaped into her mouth and she became with child. After eight months, she could hear a voice from within her womb, and, on the first day of the new year, he was born in the stable. The child was called the Prince of the Imperial Stable, or the Eight-eared Prince, because he could clearly discern each voice of a group of eight people speaking at once. Since the temple was built by this great incarnated sage, the sound of prayers echo even from the pining winds whispering in the eaves. Truly, it is a blessed sanctuary for many a holy man.

Across the sea to the west was the isle of Awaji, foaming waves dashing against its shore, and Sumiyoshi Shrine, where the restless cries of plovers allow no sleep. In ancient times, the great god Izanagi cleansed himself in the land of Hyūga, and six gods arose from the sea: Sokowatazumi, Nakawatazumi, and Utsuwatazumi, who are enshrined at Shikanoshima, and three others, Sokotsuno, Uwatsuno, and Nakatsuno, the gods of Sumiyoshi. When the empress Jingū mounted forces against the Three Kingdoms of Korea, the gods of Sumiyoshi appeared as protective deities of her vessel and enabled her easily to prevail. She built a shrine at Sumiyoshi and there made celebratory offerings. The empress Jingū is also worshiped there, and thus, while the other Sumiyoshi shrine at Nakodo shelters three deities, this Sumiyoshi shrine shelters four. Kanenari is said to have expressed its spirit:

Nishi no umi ya	Ah—the western seas!
aoki ga hara no	Out of the tidewaters
shioji yori	on an evergreen plain they appear:
awaredashi	the gods of Sumiyoshi.[15]
Sumiyoshi no kami	

Empress Jitō[16] sang of this place:

Kami yo kami	Oh ye gods!
na o Sumiyoshi to	Thy name is Sumiyoshi,
misonawase	sacred pillars of strength
waga yo ni tatsuru	upholding my reign.[17]
miyabashira nari	

And the poet Sanesada:

Sumiyoshi no	Flower festoons:
hamamatsu ga e no	faintly visible
taema yori	through branches of pine
honoka ni miyuru	on the beach of Sumiyoshi.[18]
hana no yūshide	

It was in the first year of Tennan[19] that Emperor Montoku[20] journeyed to the shores of Sumiyoshi and sang:

Ware mite mo	Long years have passed
hisashiku naruran	since I saw them last.
Sumiyoshi no	How many ages have they lingered,
kishi no himematsu	graceful pines of Sumiyoshi beach?
iku yo henuran	

Then the deity manifested himself and said:

Mutsumashi to	You know not
kimi wa shiranami	how closely we are bound:
mizugaki no	from long ago my sacred fence
hisashiki yo yori	has embraced your reign.[21]
iwai someteki	

After the shrine had become dilapidated from months and years of neglect, the deity appeared to an emperor in a dream to inform him of its state:

Yo ya samuki	Is it that the night is chill?
koromo ya usuki	Or my robes so thin?
katasogi no	Through a gap in the roof
yukiai no ma yori	is that frost setting in?[22]
shimo ya okuran	

When Ariwara no Narihira[23] made a pilgrimage to this site, he looked out over the wide expanse of water and saw the fisherfolk casting their nets in the tides, singing in rare and wonderful voices. He composed a poem on the exceptional quality of this bay:

Kari nakite	There is autumn of crying geese
kiku no hana saku	and chrysanthemums in bloom,
aki wa aredo	but for spring at the seaside
haru no umibe ni	'tis the shore at Sumiyoshi.[24]
Sumiyoshi no hama	

How wonderful it was for Anchin to see all this before his very eyes! Splashed by the waves at the bay of Sakai, he gazed out over the harbor of Uji, where the flares of the fishing boats shimmered faintly like fireflies. Thence onward he traveled to Wakanoura, where the tides lapped at the water's edge and cranes cried and circled. Offshore winds swept through the reeds, and the clouds lifted to reveal the island of Tamatsushima under a clear moon.

The god of the shrine on this island was provisionally manifested in Sotoorihime, consort of the emperor Ingyō.[25] In the second year of Ninna,[26] the emperor Kōkō had a dream in which Sotoorihime appeared, saying:

Tachikaeri	Once more in this world
mata mo kono yo ni	I leave my traces,
ato taren	returning waves of Wakanoura
mukashi koishiki	beloved long ago.[27]
Waka no ura nami	

She is worshiped as a deity of Tamatsushima and protects the Way of Poetry. Thus, Yoshitsune, the Regent of Gokyōgoku, sang:

Ika bakari	How did the bay winds
Wakanoura kaze	touch your soul
mi ni shimite	that you were moved to compose song,
mi ya hajime ken	O Lady of Tamatsushima?[28]
Tamatsushima hime	

And the Minister of the Left of Kamakura:

Yuki tsumoru	Snow-covered pine plain at Waka
Waka no matsubara	old as the falling ages,
furinikeru	how long have you guarded
iku yo henuran	the grove of Tamatsushima?[29]
Tamatsushima mori	

Anchin looked back whence he had traveled. The full tide had erased the horizon, and azure waves splashed the heavens above. Rarely had he seen such a inexpressibly lovely sight. He knew not where his journey would lead him, its end obscure as the rising spring mist. Who might have spread the linen-like cloak of white cloud clinging to the branch tips? There was no one awaiting him, and the skies of travel stretched long, ending with a lonely sleep in the squalor of a humble hut, a midnight bell tolling at his pallet.

Passing by Kimiidera, he knelt in prayer, though it boded ill.[30] He pressed on, soon passing Fujishiro, crossing over the crest of Misaka, past Uranoto, arriving at last in the district of Muro.

Part 2

Just as the evening bell was tolling the end of yet another day, Anchin stopped at a local residence to rest from the toil of his travels. This house was owned by a woman. Anchin was such an unusually handsome man that she took an immediate fancy to him and made various appeals to win him over. Anchin had no intention of complying with her desires, but acted as if he might remain.

"Please listen to me!" he said. "Ever since I was young I have lived at Kurama Temple, immersing myself in study, praising the Buddha, and imbuing my heart with the sacred teachings. I have remained chaste, free from the tethers wrought by passions of this world of birth and death, seeking naught but the shores of Nirvana. I have placed my deepest trust in the three sacred sites of Kumano and, wishing to pay homage to their gods, am making my way there. How could this chaste pilgrim possibly engage in pleasures of the flesh? It is out of the question!"

"Why must you speak so harshly? You know that karmic bonds are forged merely through sharing the shade of a tree or through drinking the same waters. What's more, the mere fact that you came to my house shows that we are linked in former lives. It is the nature of things for purity to be sullied: the moon on a dark night falls low in the sky, and so too pure water descends to the bottom of a fall. In India, Kumaraen wed the king's sister, and, as a result, the holy master Raju was born. In our own land, the Preceptor of the Morning Sun stole the wife of a doctor of astrology. As he was lying with her, the husband discovered them, and the Preceptor hurried to escape through a small door to the west. Said the husband:

Ayashiku mo	Odd indeed
nishi yori deru	that the morning sun
asahi ka na	should emerge in the west!

And the monk quickly returned:

| Tenmon no hakase | But how can he observe it, |
| ikaga miruran | the doctor of astrology? |

With this clever response, the husband's heart softened, and he forgave the transgressor.[31] With such precedents as these, how can you be so hard hearted?" she pleaded, grasping at his sleeve.

Anchin was only human and could not help but feel pity, yet he knew that he must not allow his resolve to weaken. He had been privileged to receive this human body, so dearly won, and to receive the teachings of Buddhism, so rarely encountered; moreover, he had the good fortune to be a monk. Only a devil would flout all this to engage in evil doings! And so he lied.

"You are so kind to think well of me. Even pure white thread may be dyed crimson:

Mogamigawa	As the grain raft travels
noboreba kudaru	up and down the river Mogami,
inabune no	I'm not wholly refusing. . . .[32]
ina ni wa arazu. . .	

First, however, I must be on my way to Kumano. Once my religious aims are fulfilled, I will return and share your pillow, and you and I will exchange vows of love like the waters of two streams merging into one. Please wait until then—I promise not to betray you." His tone was of the utmost sincerity.

"Wonderful! I'll be awaiting your return," responded the delighted woman.

As the cocks crowed and the eastern skies were tinged with light, Anchin departed with the mist on his way to Kumano. He arrived at the shrine complex and read sutras to gratify the gods. Kumano

surpassed his every expectation, and he marveled at all he saw. That night, he kept vigil in the Purification Hall, praying for enlightenment and deliverance from the cycle of birth and death. As the night deepened, even the shadows of the hall seemed to be suffused with holiness, and his heart was cleansed. The wind whistling through the pines swept away the mists in his heart, and the thundering Nachi Falls resounded into his dozing, awakening him from his reveries.

He saw that among the many pilgrims were a priest about fifty years old and a layman about forty, a box of wares strapped to his back. "When did the gods of this shrine first appear on the mountain?" the layman was inquiring of the priest.

"I couldn't possibly know the origins of the shrine, but I'll tell you what people say—it might stave off your drowsiness. It is said that the manifestation first appeared in this land in the reign of the emperor Kōrei,[33] when an old couple attended by two servants arrived here. When the natives asked these newcomers to identify themselves, the old man responded that he had been summoned by the people of Kii; ever since this area has been known as the province of Kii. Emperor Sujin[34] built the Main Shrine; Emperor Keikō[35] built the New Shrine. How marvelous they are! The original deity of the Main Shrine is the Savior Buddha, of the New Shrine the Healing Buddha, of Nachi the Thousand-Armed Kannon. They appear in provisional manifestations as expedient means to save all sentient beings.

"When the emperor Go Shirakawa came here and went through the thirty-three stages of the pilgrimage, the deity was manifested at a place called Mimoto, and said:

Uro yori mo	This is a Way that leads
muro ni irinuru	to purity from impurity;
michi nareba	this indeed is the gate
kore zo hotoke no	to the Buddha.
mikado naru beki	

When Izumi Shikibu came here, she was standing before the main shrine when suddenly her monthly flow began. She despondently recited:

Inishie no
goshō no kumo
hare yarade
tsuki no sawari to
naru zo kanashiki

Clouds of the Five Hindrances
yet uncleared:
how sad to be cursed
with my monthly impediment!

The god responded:

Moto yori mo
chiri ni majiwaru
kami nareba
tsuki no sawari
nani ka kurushiki

I am a god who has mingled always
with the dust of humanity.
How could I possibly be harmed
by a monthly flow?[36]

At the shrine of Awakening Gate, the provisional councillor Tsune-fusa composed:

Ureshiku mo
kami no chikai o
shirube ni te
kokoro o okosu
kado ni irinu

With great gladness
my heart roused,
guided by the vow of the god
I have entered the gate.[37]

At the shrine of Shioya, the Great Minister of the Center of Go Sanjō composed:

Omou koto
kumite kanauru
kami nareba
Shioya ni ato o
taruru narikeri

This is a god who grants
one's every desire.
Thus has he manifested
his traces at Shioya."[38]

Presently, Anchin departed the three sacred mountains and set off on his return journey.

Reckoning that he should be arriving soon, the woman prepared all kinds of rare delicacies, then went to stand by the gate and waited with ever-mounting anticipation. Yet Anchin knew that he must not stop there and so laid his plans well. He had already crept past stealthily and was soon far away.

The woman tired of her vigil and scanned the mountains intently. When a small party of mountain priests passed by on their return from Kumano, she asked if they had seen such and such a man. "A monk meeting that description left two days ago," replied one as he hurried by.

When she heard this, the woman's face changed color. "I've been tricked! How could he have been so false? How despicable! He won't escape me!" she cried, taking off in hot pursuit.

By this time, Anchin had arrived at Hidaka village and was resting under a tree. When he glanced back at the road he had traveled, to his shock and terror the woman emerged into view. Desperate for a hiding place, he ran to the temple of Dōjōji and explained his plight to the monks, begging them for assistance. They took pity on him and debated what they might do. One old man stepped forward and said, "We can't waste precious time discussing this. Why don't we lower the bell and hide him inside?" All the monks agreed to this plan, and together they managed to lower the bell. Once Anchin was safely concealed within, they carefully sealed off the bell tower.

Dōjōji was built by Lord Tachibana no Michinari; hence it is called Dōjōji.[39]

In no time at all, the woman arrived at the village of Hidaka. Without warning, the waters of the river rose enormously high. Great waves crashed at the shore, making it impossible for her to cross, and she ran back and forth praying for the flood to subside. Suddenly she was transformed into a great serpent, able to swim across easily.

Soon she reached the temple and searched everywhere, but could not find the object of her desire. As she was frantically dashing about, she discovered that the bell tower had been cordoned off. She stared at it with suspicion, then lashed at the tower with her tail, smashing it to pieces. Taking the bell loop between her fangs, she wrapped herself seven times around the bell. Spitting flames of furious venom, she lashed at it with her tail. Soon sparks flew and the bell grew red hot. The serpent's eyeballs gleamed like two suns

rising in the sky, two horns like withered branches sprang out of her head, and sharp fangs like black iron protruded from her jaw. She flicked her crimson tongue and slithered into the Hidaka River. All who witnessed this were frightened out of their wits and scrambled to escape.

Afterward, the priests gathered to discuss this strange and terrible event. They overturned the bell and saw that the flesh of the monk had been so burnt by the smoke of those raging flames that only parched bones remained behind. The grieving holy men collected the remains and read sutras and incantations over them. This kind of occurance is not without precedent. In Kamakura, the daughter of a certain man so loved the young acolyte of a priest of Wakamiya Temple that she fell ill. She told her mother of her passion, and the mother informed the young man's parents, who had the boy visit the girl. He felt no desire for her, though, and her condition worsened until finally she died. Her grieving father and mother put her ashes in a box for eventual interment at Zenkō Temple. After her death, the acolyte himself became ill. As his malady worsened, his parents moved him to a small room better to nurse him, but there seemed to be no hope for recovery. On one occasion, the parents heard voices conversing in the room; thinking it strange, they peered through a crack. To their horror, they saw the son conversing with a large serpent. Soon the boy died, and after the funeral services it was discovered that a serpent had entwined itself around the body so inextricably that the body had to be buried as it was. When the girl's parents made preparations to send her remains to Zenkō Temple, they opened the box in order to retain some of the ashes at a local temple. Inside, they found that some of the bones had changed wholly into small snakes, and other bones were half transformed.[40]

In truth, nothing is more dreadful than love and attachment. It is difficult indeed to dispell the effects of passion in this drifting world of birth and death. How terrible it is!

Part 3

The bell of Dōjōji had been silenced. No more could its tolling awaken its listeners from the slumber of spiritual darkness. The priests unanimously decided to have another bell cast. To everyone's delight, they succeeded easily, and an auspicious day was chosen for the dedication ceremony. On the appointed day, all the local folk thronged into the compound, so tightly packed that sleeve brushed against sleeve and heel wedged against heel, in order not to miss the ceremonies. The priests were gratified at the huge attendance, but directed the head custodian[41] to announce that women were forbidden to attend the dedication.

"Why is that?" he asked.

"You know what happened here before, so take the utmost caution and be on your guard."

"I understand," he replied, and selected his assistants. As they were hoisting the bell, there appeared a beautiful woman about twenty years old, carrying a red fan. She pushed through the crowd of workers and entered the courtyard of the main hall.

"Hey!" cried the custodian. "You, woman! Women are strictly forbidden at the ceremonies. There was a sign posted at the gate— why have you come this far? Leave the temple! Quickly, before I throw you out!"

"I am a dancer from this province," she responded. "I heard that there was to be a bell dedication and wanted to attend. I was so happy! I thought that if I could just hear the bell, the clouds of the Five Hindrances[42] would be cleared. I've come so far . . . please let me in! I'll dance for you at the dedication."

"What an agreeable woman you are! It's strictly forbidden, but go ahead and dance. I am in charge of the ceremonies; quickly, come this way."

The woman seemed to be delighted. "Then I shall dance," she announced and, donning her hat and costume, began to stamp out the beat. Then she rose and rhythmically intoned:

"Apart from the flowers, the wind in the pines echoes fiercely.
Those who harken to the tolling of this temple bell are awakened from the dreams of 108 afflictions.
The first evening bell tolls the impermanence of all things.
The second bell tolls the law of extinguishment of all life.
Until the dawn, all life and death are quenched in Nirvana.
The dawn bell echoes the tranquility of Nirvana and gives rise to the path of the Enlightened one. . . .
King Keinida of India was a demon of evil karma who killed thousands. The burden of his sins caused the earth to cleave asunder, and, still alive, he descended into hell. His neck was wedged

between two daggers and his head cut off. He was about to die, but revived, only to be beheaded yet again. The Buddha took pity on him and bade a disciple to ring a bell. As long as it echoed, Keinida's neck remained whole, and thus his suffering was momentarily eased. Keisō of China trangressed a sacred law, died, and fell into hell. As he was subjected to innumerable torments, he perceived the sound of the bell of Kakanji and was saved from suffering. When the Buddha was preaching at Vulture Peak, the rich man Shudatsu[43] cast a bell and had it hung there, ringing it when the Buddha spoke, and thus all gathered to hear. The eight great dragon kings also ascended the mountain, accompanied by their many followers. There were Nanda, Batsunanda, Shagara, Washukitsu, Tokushaka, Arabadatta, Manashi, and Ubara.[44] As they listened to the Buddha speak, they wept tears of joy. Was this not a blessing of the bell?

I have been drawn to this bell . . . if I could but hear the sound of the Law, then, like the dragon princess, I too might attain Buddhahood. Oh joy of joys! Nothing could be greater than that!

The clear silhouette of the moon descends,
birds sing and frost fills the sky, against white flowers.
Everyone is asleep, and opportunity draws nigh
for the fulfillment of my passionate desire. . . ."

As she continued to dance, she circled the bell and tried to grasp onto it.

"Now I remember! I hate this bell!" she cried, grabbing onto the bell loop. She leaped up, pulled the bell over her, and disappeared within.[45]

The astonished crowd raised a wave of murmurs. The bell grew hot; then a sudden wind gusted, and rain pelted down. Lightning flashed from among the clouds, and thunder rumbled. The priests gathered in the courtyard to decide what to do. One stepped forward and said, "That woman is still here in this temple and once again is trying to harm the bell. Our Buddhist rituals should dispel her—let us pray to raise the bell."

"You are right. Indeed, we must," agreed the others. "Though the sands of the Hidaka River run out, the power of the law of our brotherhood can never weaken.

In the East, oh Gozanze, the Guardian King!
In the South, oh Gundari, the Guardian King!
In the West, oh Daitoku, the Guardian King!
In the North, oh Kongo Yasha, the Guardian King!
In the Center, oh Immovable Guardian King!
Will the bell move?
Mandabasaranan senda makaroshana sowataya untaratakanman.[46]
Those who hear my words shall gain wisdom.
Those who know my heart shall become buddhas in this life."

Now that they had prayed for the serpent's salvation, how could it bear any malice toward them? The dawn moon struck the hanging bell, and it began to move.

"All together, pray!"

The priests invoked the sacred spell of the Thousand-Armed Kannon and the spell for salvation through the compassion of the Immovable Flaming Guardian King. So fiercely did they pray that black smoke rose; so vehement were their prayers that the bell resounded, though struck by no one, and danced, though pulled by no one. Soon it rose to the bell tower, and the shape of a serpent appeared. The priests prayed with renewed vigor.

We beseech the Green Dragon of the East.
We beseech the White Dragon of the West.
We beseech the Yellow Dragon of the Center.
Dragon kings of the Great Triple Thousand Worlds, whose numbers are as the sands of the Ganges! Have mercy and hear our prayers![47]

Defeated by their prayers, the serpent fell with a crash, but arose once again. "Oh, how I hate you," she spat at the bell. Her fiery breath scorched the bell tower, but the priests quelled the flames with the holy sign of fragrant water. The great serpent roused the waves of the Hidaka River, parted the waters, and entered within.

Their prayers fulfilled, the gratified priests took hold of the bell hammer and rang the bell. In that sound echoed the impermanence of all things; indeed, it might have been the tolling of the

crystal bell in the Impermanence Hall of Gion Temple.[48] Those who heard it were awakened from their slumber of birth and death; everyone, men and women alike, from within and without the temple, gathered to listen. All agreed that the flourishing of the Buddhist law was wholly due to the blessing of this bell.

Some time later, the priests had a dream in which two large serpents appeared. "I am that monk inside the bell," said one, "and this is the woman. Although in my lifetime I clung steadfastly to the Lotus Sutra, I met with this unhappy fate. Please copy out the Chapter on the Lifespan from the Lotus Sutra and dedicate it on my behalf." Then the dream ended.

Moved by his plight, the priests held memorial services, offered incense and flowers in the main hall, and copied the prescribed chapter from the sutra. That night, the monk and woman appeared once again in their dreams. "We are so grateful to you! Thanks to the power of the sutra, this monk has been reborn in the Tushita heaven, and the woman has been reborn in the Toriten heaven." Then this dream of the brightly shining heavens ended.

The eight scrolls of the wondrous Lotus Sutra represent the original desire of the Enlightened Buddha and are a direct path through which all sentient beings may attain enlightenment. The reason is stated in the sutra itself, in the Chapter on Expedient Means: "Change all sentient beings for the better and allow them to enter the Buddha's path." This phrase means that the Original Desire of the Shakamuni Buddha is fulfilled through recitation of the Lotus Sutra. Virtuous people attain the way through their practices, but evildoers cannot attain buddhahood. Heavenly beings and those who practice good acts may attain deliverance, but animals and fighting spirits may not. However, through this wondrous sutra, all beings—those in hell, hungry ghosts, animals, fighting spirits, humans, and heavenly beings alike—may be drawn to the path, and the Buddha's vow shall be everlasting.

Thanks to the prayers of so many holy men, the monk and woman were able to break free of their serpentine forms and to achieve rebirth in heaven. All this was due to the blessing of the Lotus Sutra.

NOTES

1. For a translation of the *Konjaku monogatari shū*, see Ury, *Tales of Times Now Past*, pp. 93–96. For the *Hokekyōkenki*, see Yoshiko K. Dykstra, *Miraculous Tales of the Lotus Sutra from Ancient Japan* (Honolulu:

University of Hawaii Press, 1983), pp. 145–146. For the *Ugetsu monogatari*, see Leon Zolbrod, trans., *Ugetsu Monogatari: Tales of Moonlight and Rain* (London: George Allen & Unwin, 1974. Reprint. Rutland, Vt. and Tokyo: Chas. E. Tuttle, 1977), pp. 161–184.

2. This passage about the elephant and the deer echoes almost verbatim sec. 9 of Kenkō's *Tsurezuregusa*. See Donald Keene, trans., *Essays in Idleness* (New York: Columbia University Press, 1967), p. 9.

3. This is the subject of the nō play *Ikkaku Sennin*. When the hermit fell in love, all the rain dragons were released, ending a long draught.

4. Related in episode 37 of the *Taiheiki (Chronicle of the Great Peace)*.

5. An important pilgrimage site at the tip of the Kii Peninsula, Kumano actually consisted of three geographically proximate shrines: the Hongū (Main Shrine), Shingū (New Shrine), and Nachi. These three form one entity as the center of a syncretic Shinto-Buddhist belief system.

6. This is a rewording of *Senzaishū* no. 494.

7. This poem appears in the anthology *Shūishū* no. 1342. It is said to have been Izumi Shikibu's deathbed poem.

8. This poem appears in *Tōren hōshi shū* no. 58 *(Collection of Poetry by Priest Tōren)*, in the poetic compendium *Zoku Kokka taikan*.

9. Episode 82 of *The Tales of Ise (Ise monogatari)* relates that Prince Koretaka had a villa here, to which he brought hunting parties for amusement.

10. Takaradera.

11. This famous account of the poet-priest Saigyō is recounted in the nō play *Eguchi*. The poem itself appears in several sources, including Saigyō's collection, the *Sankashū*.

12. Shitennōji, in the center of present-day Ōsaka.

13. The Four Heavenly Kings are Tammuten, Jikokuten, Zojoten, and Komukuten.

14. Reigned 585–587.

15. *Zoku kokinshū* no. 751.

16. Reigned 690–697.

17. *Zoku kokinshū* no. 738.

18. *Shinkokinshū* no. 1913.

19. 857.

20. Reigned 850–858.

21. This exchange constitutes episode 117 of *The Tales of Ise*.

22. *Shinkokinshū* no. 1855.

23. Identified as "the man of old" in *The Tales of Ise*. Also referred to in *The Tale of the Brazier* and *Old Lady Tokiwa*.

24. This poem appears in episode 68 of *The Tales of Ise*.

25. Reigned 423–453.

26. 886.

27. Sotoorihime is said to have excelled at poetry *(waka)* and thus is identified with the Bay of Waka. The source of the poem is unknown.

28. *Zoku kokinshū* no. 729.

29. The author, Minamoto no Sanetomo, was the third Kamakura shōgun; the poem appears in his personal collection, the *Kinkai waka shū.*

30. Kimiidera is the second of thirty-three temples on a pilgrimage route. A primary position is associated with wisdom, a secondary position with foolishness; hence, Kimiidera is linked with stupidity.

31. This anecdote appears in the *Shasekishū,* 7:1.

32. The monk is quoting the first four lines from a poem ending in *kono tsuki bakari* (for this month only), indicating that he will fulfill her desires at a later time. This poem is used in the same way in *The Errand Woman.*

33. Reigned 290–215 B.C.E.

34. Reigned 97 B.C.E.–30 C.E.

35. Reigned 71–130.

36. This and the preceeding account of the emperor Go Shirakawa are related in the *Fugashū* anthology, nos. 2098 and 2099, respectively. *The Tale of Dōjōji* cites slightly different versions of the first and second poems from those of the anthology. In both cases, I have retained the text's versions. In the first, the *Fugashū* gives *Mimoto* in place of *mikado* (gate); in Izumi Shikibu's poem, the *Fugashū* version reads: "Hare yaranu / mi no ukigumo no / tanabikite / tsuki no sawari to / naru zo kanashiki" (Because menstruation was thought to be impure, menstruating women were forbidden to enter sacred spaces).

37. *Kin'yoshū* no. 1265.

38. *Senzaishū* no. 1255.

39. This line is a vestige of the Dōjōji engi, which seeks to explain the history and origin of the temple. Read according to the Chinese pronunciation, *Michinari* becomes *Dōjō; ji* means "temple."

40. This anecdote is almost identical to one in the setsuwa collection *Shasekishū,* 7:2.

41. *Nōriki,* a member of the ecclesiastical community in charge of projects requiring great physical labor.

42. *Goshō.* See *The Tale of the Brazier,* n. 6.

43. Sudatta.

44. This passage is condensed from the Japanese text, which contains a long list of the names and alternate names of the dragon kings as well as brief descriptions of each, no doubt once functioning as an incantation.

45. Parts of the passage commencing with the woman's dance resemble portions of the nō *Dojōji.* It is likely that this latter third of *The Tale of*

Dōjōji was written with direct reference to contemporary dramatic performance librettos of the Dōjōji story.

46. A mystical incantation *(darani).*

47. Much of pt. 3 resembles the latter half of the nō *Dōjōji.* The passage comprising the priests' prayers is almost identical to the corresponding section of that play and may have been transcribed from it.

48. The Jetavana Monastery in India.

The King of Farts
Fukutomi chōja monogatari

The King of Farts (Fukutomi chōja monogatari—lit., "The Tale of Rich Man Windfall") is a cautionary tale, product of an age abounding in overnight millionaires and abject poverty. It is known in Japanese art circles through its more famous antecedent, the Kamakura period *Fukutomi zōshi* illustrated scroll set, which relates the good fortune of a virtuous man in the first scroll and the comeuppance of his would-be imitator in the second. *The King of Farts* is based on this second scroll. It is unclear whether it was a deliberate adaptation or whether the copyist had only this scroll for his reference. In either case, unlike the earlier *Fukutomi zōshi*, which features sparse lines of dialogue accompanying numerous illustrations, *The King of Farts* is a genuine extended narrative.

Much of the humor of this scatological farce is derived from the incongruity of an art of farting and a poor man's misguided attempts at emulation. It is not particularly unseemly, for Windfall Oribe, the "Master Farter," to make his living from flatulation: entertainment of this nature was probably one of the many grotesque curiosities of medieval street shows and carnivals. Yet certainly the text is also making an ironic comment on the medieval concept of *michi,* whereby the practice of an art was seen as a means of spiritual elevation. In the text, Windfall speaks of his farting as michi, and he is accorded the same degree of respect given to a master of the esteemed art of poetry. Of course, Windfall has done no work to develop his art; he was merely lucky. When his neighbor Tōda leaps at the chance for instant proficiency, he receives a hard lesson in self-reliance. Both characters represent a travesty of the rule of slow accretion of skill in tandem with spiritual advancement, just as the skill itself is a travesty of more refined arts.

This translation is based on the annotated text printed in *Otogi-zōshi,* ed. Ichiko Teiji (pp. 385–392). The original manuscript is an illustrated scroll in the collection of the Dai Tokyū Memorial Library, which has kindly provided the illustrations. The scribe, Naoume, is otherwise unknown.

One should never envy the good fortune of another, for it may not accord with one's own lot in life. Long ago there lived a rich man known as Windfall Oribe,[1] who, thanks to some sort of favorable karma accrued in the past, possessed a particular inborn art at which he displayed uncanny ability without the need for practice. He achieved great fame effortlessly and was looked on as a god incarnate. His art was extremely vulgar, so everyone from all walks of life was familiar with it; since it was humorous, even the aristocracy came to hear of it and summoned him to perform to their vast amusement. Thereupon Windfall's wealth and happiness grew in leaps and bounds. He raised ridgepole upon ridgepole and built storehouse after storehouse. In his gardens, the five grains[2] sprang up lushly without the need for human cultivation.

Next door to Windfall lived a poor man named Hard-up Tōda.[3] Here, in marked contrast to the prosperity of his neighbor, smoke never rose from the chimney, and a tangle of weeds choked the path to the door. There was only a thatched fence instead of an earthen wall and rush blinds in place of curtains. In winter, his cold pallet provided scant comfort, and, since the fencing and eaves had been plundered long ago for firewood to ease the night chill, the

icy winds of winter blew in all the more. In summer, Hard-up wore shabby hempen robes and swatted away mosquitoes with a battered fan. Thus he lived day in and day out, the moonflowers growing near the eaves providing his only solace. When he was quite young, he had married a woman at least ten years his senior, whose enormous gaping mouth earned her the nickname Old Harpy.[4]

One day Old Harpy confronted her husband and said, "Even an idler without a profession, who belongs to none of the four classes, can be known far and wide and make his way up in the world if he has just one real art to display. Ah, it's just too cruel! You must not have been pious enough in an earlier life to have been born into this one without a single talent. It's truly a shame, such a shame!

"You may not be able to read or write, play an instrument, or dance, but there's no good reason why you can't learn that one art of our neighbor Windfall. Get yourself on over there, beg for lessons, and practice your heart out. Treat him as your master, and become his disciple. Miracles can happen in this world! Why, even if you don't become as famous as he, at least you'll be able to get by. And, if you're really clever at it, we here can have riches equal to theirs. He has a natural talent, to be sure, but you can't maintain an art without practice. As they say, polishing brings out the shine in a jewel. Anyway, learn it! If you don't, I'm sorry to say that you'll have to let your old lady go. With this fresh shining face of mine, I could have my choice of men." On and on she nagged.

Hard-up gave in to her arguments. He went next door and bowed obsequiously, saying one thing and another. Windfall came out to greet him. "Welcome, welcome! Yes, I'm aware of how you people over there exist from day to day, and I'm terribly sorry for you. I wanted to invite you to be my student and tell you that I was willing to be your master, but one shouldn't presume to offer advice in such matters. So time slipped by without my going on over to encourage you." He went on in a very sympathetic and friendly manner.

Hard-up bowed deeply and beamed. "My, my, this certainly is kind of you. Old Harpy has been after me constantly, but I never imagined that you would share such a glorious accomplishment as yours with any other family, so I ignored her advice. Now I regret having wasted the past few years. When I tell her how very gracious you've been, it will please her to no end," he groveled, hands pressed together reverently.

Windfall's ire was aroused by this new assault of obsequiousness. With malice in his heart, he told Tōda, "Well, to practice my art you must first take a precious medicine before you perform—don't tell anyone about it! This is a family secret, so be sure that you never tell a soul!" Producing what seemed to be an old scroll, he explained in great detail how to prepare the ingredients.

"You've already been most generous, but would you mind giving me enough of that esteemed compound for just one performance? Old Harpy has been bossing and scolding me so much that I need to blow a few right away to show her what I can do," Hard-up pleaded fervently.

"In that case. . . ." Windfall entered his house and returned with two round black pills.[5] "These are not to be taken on an empty stomach. Prepare your stomach with lots of food, then, exactly four hours before you expect to perform, wash them down with warm salt water. You're guaranteed to be a sensation! Don't worry if they don't take effect immediately, but, if it seems to take too long, scoop some water into a tub, dunk in your behind, and hold your breath," he instructed carefully.

Hard-up was delighted. He took his leave and returned home, raising the pills to his brow in gratitude. Old Harpy was waiting impatiently. "Well? Well? Did you learn anything? Did he teach you anything?"

Grinning with delight, Hard-up related what had happened. His wife was overjoyed. "This very day, call on a person of consequence," she urged. "Announce yourself loudly and clearly, saying 'I am Tōda, a disciple of Windfall Oribe. I will blast them out in any way you desire.' I'd like to hear a trial run beforehand, but there are only two pills, and it would be a pity to waste them. Hurry up and get going!"

From a wicker trunk by the corner of the door she removed an old court hat, a persimmon-colored cloak, a pale blue overcloak, and a pair of wide trousers and dressed him up. "Don't drag your feet! Go in with your spine straight and your chin held high!" She brushed the dust from the hat, slicked back his hair, looked at his front, then circled around to inspect the back. "With that hat on you look just like you did when you came to my parents' house to marry me. My, my, you're such a gentleman, such a gentleman!"

Hard-up took the tablets as instructed and set off. As he walked along, his stomach lurched and roared like thunder, but he tightened his buttocks and hurried on. The Honorable Middle Captain of Imadegawa was said to be a young man who might be amused by this sort of entertainment; he might reward Hard-up with all kinds of gifts. Hard-up arrived at the Middle Captain's residence and announced himself to the lord's retainers. The Middle Captain was interested: things had been rather boring of late, and he had tired of his studies. He ordered Hard-up to the garden, seated him on a straw mat by the side of the courtyard, and treated him to a lavish spread of food and wine. Then he sat expectantly with his ear cocked. Behind a reed screen inside were assembled his younger sister, who served at court, his cloistered grandmother, and his wife.

Hard-up's stomach hurt, but he tried to concentrate on the food. How odd! How dreadful! His guts were cramping, and his stomach was in such spasms that he could bear the pain no longer and tried to leave.

Just then, he abruptly let loose a spray as powerful as a water spout, leaving the white pebbled courtyard looking as if it had been covered by a scattering of primrose petals. He was musing that the mansions in Ide might look something like this[6] when a sudden breeze arose, wafting the stench all over the palace. It was disgusting, to say the least. Hard-up pressed together his reddened buttocks and prepared to flee, but the servants and houseboys leaped down brandishing whips and beat him until he was prone. He stuck out his bruised rear end and wailed; then they pulled him up by his hat and topknot and chased him out of the courtyard.

Blood flowed from the gashes on his forehead and trickled down to the ground in a stream as crimson as the autumn foliage along the Tatsuta River.[7] Smashed court hat perched on his head like a snail's shell, blood seeping through his sleeves and hem, he slowly made his way home. How mortifying a figure he cut in broad daylight! Children playing hide-and-go-seek and blindman's bluff pointed and laughed as he passed by. Hard-up's battered haunches and skinned knees were excruciatingly painful; he wanted to sit and rest on the stoop of a shop, but he smelled so foul that no one would allow him to come near. He was quite a sight as he crept home, dragging his tail behind him.

Meanwhile, Old Harpy had been waiting by the gate all afternoon, impatiently craning her neck to watch the road. She spied him approaching from over two blocks away and thought to herself, "Aha! There's a crowd of people around him; they must be escorting him home. I'll bet the nobles really liked him!"[8] As he drew closer, she waxed ecstatic, thinking that he had been outfitted in a new red robe. All the more impatient, she dashed inside, crying, "Our old clothes are so ugly! Now that we're bound to be rich, I certainly won't wear rags like these! Why should the children[9] have to wear them either?" She tore the robes off the clothespole, fanned the fire, and burned them to ashes. Her grandson cried out in protest, but she paid no attention. Her daughter-in-law was caught up in the excitement, but waited agoggle still half in disbelief.[10]

Hard-up painfully arrived home. What had appeared to be the crimson of a new robe was in fact blood from his head, and his now bright yellow trousers were sagging and dripping. Since he could touch no one, he was leaning on a stick, nose crusted over, face fixed in a scowl. He was utterly miserable. Any change of clothing had been reduced to ashes, so he stripped naked, hugging his shoulders in silence, shaking and shivering, his balls hanging down darkly. All in all, he looked as down and out as his name suggested.

The nun Myōsai from the house to the north called to express her sympathy. "Words fail me! Hail Amida Buddha!" she cried, and beat a hasty retreat. The mistress of the house next door[11] peered with pity through the slats of her blind, staring at his nether regions.

All that night and the following day his stomach ached. Evening mist rose from his behind, and it seemed that nocturnal insects were chirping in his guts. His bowels emptied like rain from autumn skies, fitfully stopping and starting. Racked by spasms of diarrhea, he moaned and groaned in pain. Old Harpy was furious, but she was hardly in a position to utter a word of reproach. When she warmed her wrinkled hands and tried to massage his stomach, such a smell arose that it was difficult to do anything at all, so she laid him out flat on his face and, grabbing onto the clothespole for balance, walked up and down his spine. The grandson shook with delighted laughter. "Pee pee! It's dripping!" Old Harpy saw that he was wet from the small of his back down to his heels and realized that his malady was yet unabated. His daughter-in-law brought great quantities of hot water, but he would not so much as glance at it. Oh, how it hurt! How it hurt!

Hard-up grew weaker and weaker as the days and nights passed. He couldn't even negotiate the path[12] to the toilet now, but instead would put on high clogs, weave his way out to the garden, and, leaning on the fulling stone, spray out large quantities of liquid. His throat was parched, and he would cry pitifully for water just like a child, but soon lost whatever he could wash down. In time he grew terribly thin; his formerly round face became gaunt, and his sunken eyes were wreathed in black rings.

Thinking that his very life hung in the balance, his wife went to the office of Kiyomaro, the Head of the Bureau of Physicians. Plaintively she told her tale, pleading that a compassionate man distinguishes not rich from poor. The physician met with her and gave her some medicine, and at last she was able to breathe a sigh of relief.

She was still angry at Windfall, however. Going out to the river-bank, she purified herself, cut out paper for a prayer wand, faced south, and prayed. "Hear me! I follow the Law and pay homage to the Buddha. Oh, ye three deities of Kumano! Take that Windfall Oribe, who has so shamed my husband, into your power and make him suffer!" She rubbed her prayer beads furiously and prayed for evil to befall her enemy. She must have been heard, for a large-billed bird came flying from the direction of Kumano, dipped its wings over the stick, and sang. She returned home confident that her request would be granted.[13]

When she realized that Windfall must have deliberately deceived her husband, her hatred flared tenfold. "Somehow I'll take my revenge," she thought, waiting feverishly day and night.

It is the way of the world that one must bear the weight of another's grievances.[14] Windfall was afflicted with continual nightmares. He consulted a soothsayer, who advised him to declare a taboo for seven days, fasten shut his gate, and see no one. This was so dreary a prospect that Windfall decided to ask the gods to reverse his ill fortune. He set off on a pilgrimage the very next morning. Old Harpy caught wind of his journey and waited at the roadside for his return. As soon as he appeared, she seized him fiercely with the wild look of a mountain demon. How terribly frightful! Since Windfall was a man, he was able to wrench away from her grip and flee, but she chased after him, clamped her teeth down on his chest, and shook her head back and forth more savagely than a rabid dog. Her eyeballs rolled upside down, and her mouth split open to the ears, just like a furious serpent. Passersby cried out, "It's a people-eating demon! How awful!" Some ran away, and others stayed to gawk in fascination.

Two itinerant minstrels named Tameichi and Utaichi, shuffling

sleepily down the road on their return from an overnight vigil, were startled awake by all the commotion. Imagining that it came from wild beasts, they took to their heels as fast as they could. The Lord Chamberlain thought that the mad barking of the dogs meant that a thief was about. He picked up a small bow and went out to shoot the culprit, but, on hearing the cries "Demon, demon!" returned home quietly.

And that's what happened long ago.

Autumn 1750
Transcribed by Naoume

NOTES

1. Fukutomi no Oribe. I have freely translated *fukutomi* (wealth and prosperity) as "windfall," intentionally punning on the nature of his profession. *Fuku* also means "to blow"; perhaps his name incorporates this pun.

2. Wheat, rice, beans, and two kinds of millet.

3. Bokushō no Tōda. *Bokushō* is composed of two characters, denoting "poor" and "sparse."

4. *Oniuba*, lit., "old lady demon." Demons were imagined to have large mouths.

5. In the *Fukutomi zōshi* scrolls, the "medicine" is described as ground-up morning glory seeds.

6. A location famed for the beauty of its primroses *(yamabuki).*

7. The picture caption reads: "A poor farter makes this kind of uproar. / Beat him! Beat him! / Could he have been drunk? / It has the stink of a rotten persimmon. / It reeks! It reeks!"

8. The picture caption reads: "People peeked out from roadside stalls and snickered. / Look at that! Don't do poo-poo, little boy! / What a stink—you'd think the great wind god himself let it out!"

9. The text specifically states "daughter-in-law and grandson." Nothing is mentioned about a son.

10. The picture caption reads: "Oh, how it smoked! / She must have loved that smoke—that billowing smoke. / Stand back! Stand back!"

11. Perhaps Windfall's wife?

12. The text reads *michi,* another satirical reference to the exalted "way."

13. I have corrected an inversion of this and the preceding paragraph in the Japanese text. Ichiko Teiji, the annotator of the text, believes that the copyist must have blundered.

14. The original—"Hito no nageki wa ou naru yo no naka"—is unclear.

A Tale of Two Nursemaids

Menoto no sōshi

Like many otogi-zōshi, *A Tale of Two Nursemaids* represents the fusion of two separate genres in a single narrative: here, a letter of advice to a young lady and a lengthy frame story situating the letter within a humorous context. The frame story is patterned after the contrastive parable of good and evil so common to the Japanese folktale. It describes two girls raised by two wholly different nurses, one the embodiment of ladylike virtues, the other coarse and mean spirited. While the tale is as humorous to the modern Western reader as it must have been to a medieval Japanese, it is important to recognize that the two audiences would perceive the humor quite differently. The modern reader is likely to sympathize with the eccentric nurse and her charge and see in the narrative feminist themes quite alien to medieval Japan. The medieval reader would have been amused by the incongruity of an aristocratic young lady learning mathematics or strumming a lute like a blind minstrel. For the original audience, the lighthearted manner with which the story treated a serious subject by no means detracted from the weight of its message; this is a story that reaffirmed rather than disrupted traditional values.

The letter occupying most of the latter half of the story was probably adapted from an admonitory epistle known as *Niwa no oshie (Domestic Teachings)* or its variant, the *Menoto no fumi (A Nursemaid's Letter)*, attributed to the poetess and nun Abutsu (d. 1283).[1] Reputedly written as a guide to court customs and etiquette prompted by the court debut of the author's own daughter, it is an early manifestation of that genre of didactic works devoted to inculcating appropriate values and behavior in women, represented by such later works as the Edo period *Onna daigaku (Great Teaching for Women)*.

This translation is based on the unannotated text printed in Ichiko Teiji, ed., *Mikan chūsei shōsetsu* 2 (Koten bunko, 1948, pp. 45–78), transcribed from an undated, unillustrated manuscript in the collection of the Tokyo University Library. The only other extant manuscript, tentatively dated late Muromachi, is in a private collection. Ichiko coined the present title; the original is titled only "Not so very long ago . . ." *(naka goro no koto)* after the opening line of the text. The Japanese text contains numerous passages of quoted speech that once must have served as captions to illustrations, even though the manuscript as it now exists is not illustrated. These vestigial captions are important enough to merit treatment within the main narrative of the English translation. Each such incorporation is identified in the notes.

Not so very long ago, there lived a Minister of the Left named Masahira who served during an illustrious imperial reign. This minister had two daughters. The girls were raised well enough until they reached the ages of five and six, but, the wealthier and more prosperous the Minister became, the more time he devoted to amusing himself at poetry, linked verse, and all sorts of seasonal diversions, pursuing entertainment through the blossoms of spring and maple leaves of autumn. His wife joined him in these amusements, never bothering to teach her daughters even the basics of handwriting, and thus they were left wholly in the care of their nursemaids.

The elder daughter's nurse was obese and ill tempered. She paid no heed to the admonishments of others, but arrogantly did just as she pleased. In contrast, the younger daughter's nurse was even tempered, well versed in *The Tale of Genji* and *The Tale of Sagoromo*,[2] the arts of koto, lute, and poetry, and all sorts of accomplishments necessary to elegant diversion. The Minister and his lady felt completely at ease entrusting their daughter's upbringing to this nurse, but, when they considered the merits of the other, they wondered why the elder girl was so inferior to her sister.

"I may not have any accomplishments, but not once in all these years have I ever gone hungry," said the nurse in self-defense. "My appetite is good, and I love food and drink, not to mention all kinds of bitter, salty, and sweet flavors. Just give me something edible, and watch me eat it! I love drinking tea and wine. People say that my manners are bad and my looks even worse, but I could still have my pick of any number of men. I may not be a mistress of any fancy arts, but I do know when to scratch an itch. It's pretty funny that some people call me utterly despicable because getting money and food is also an accomplishment, you know."

And she continued to rear her charge just as she pleased. She would serve meals without so much as a tray or attendants and offered fish whole and uncut. After feeding the young lady and her own child, she would then take the leftover bones for herself, crunching on them like a dog. It was just as if she were rearing a baby boar.

The nanny of the younger daughter taught her charge such refinements as calligraphy and old verse and passed the leisure hours making lovely dolls for the girl's amusement. She remained in faithful and constant attendance, always correcting the girl when she was naughty, and, by the time the young lady was ten, she had matured beautifully.

"Did you write this?" the nurse would say. "If you do your calligraphy practice nicely, I'll make you a beautiful doll."[3]

The elder daughter was called the Lady of the East, the younger the Lady of the West. All who set eyes on the nurse of the Lady of the East were terrified, vowing that they had never seen anyone quite so frightening. Thus she came to be known as the Dragon King. Also serving in the palace was a malicious gossip of a woman nicknamed the She-devil. This woman liked to visit the Lady of the East and criticize her sister to the west, then take off to the western wing, where she would speak ill of the Lady of the East.

The Dragon King had no problem with spreading tales about others but took quick offense when gossip centered on her own self. The She-devil took great pleasure in stirring up trouble and threw caution to the winds as she scurried back and forth between the two quarters. She usually stayed in the elder sister's apartments, so the Dragon King thought of her as a personal servant and confided in her without reserve.

"The Lady of the West spends all her time at calligraphy and poetry," taunted the She-devil.

"It's more than sufficient for most people to make an entry in an account book!" responded the Dragon King. "You listen too, my young lady. Doing nothing but writing poems and such won't fill an empty stomach, nor will it earn you a red cent or a single grain of rice. I'll teach you how to keep accounts and do sums; most people can't manage that!" And she wasted no time in starting the lessons.

"Look here: two times nine is eighteen."

"I see—does that mean twice nine?" asked the girl.

"That there is thirty-six."

"Four times nine is thirty-six."

"How well you catch on! No matter how skilled a bookkeeper your future husband might be, you'll always be able to hold your own. This is much better than wasting your time at painting, flower gathering, poetry, or calligraphy! Now this is really an accomplishment!"

"Just as your nurse says," added the She-devil, "it's a good skill to have."

"Never mind what those gossips over there might say, I'm teaching her a great art over here," said the Dragon King.

"Just as I always say. Where did you learn to do sums like that?"

"When I was mistress to a bookkeeper."

"I wonder who will tell her father about these lessons. It's certain that they'll manage to say nothing good about you! It makes me angry just to think about it!" said the She-devil.[4]

What with the She-devil going around dropping carefully aimed artless remarks, it stood to reason that word of the Dragon King and her doings spread everywhere.

The She-devil then proceeded to the apartments of the Lady of the West.

"The Dragon King has taught her young lady sums! Isn't that just appalling? I wouldn't have told you if it weren't the truth," she remarked maliciously.

This nursemaid paid no heed, but, feigning absorption in the koto lesson, kept her eyes steadily fixed on her pupil. She knew that she had only to respond to this evil person's tales for her words to be twisted and repeated elsewhere. Whenever the She-devil came to visit, this nurse carefully avoided confrontation and maintained her composure quite admirably.

"Now, play this in the court mode," said the nurse. "But first you must play all five modes. If you are mistaken in any one of them, you'll end up with a muddy sound. You must take great care with the bridge of your instrument."

"Should I pluck the fifth and tenth strings?" asked the girl.

"She's teaching sums over there," persisted the She-devil. "The Dragon King is very pleased and says that the young lady learns splendidly. One really should take care that ladies learn only elegant pursuits. What a disgrace!'"⁵

Returning once again to the eastern wing, the She-devil announced, "I've been to the western wing, and the nursemaid over there says, 'Is she really teaching her to do sums? How awful! Is that her idea of educating a young lady? That's just something that bookkeepers do. Who would do that?' Then she picked up a koto and laughed at you, asking why you didn't teach something like that, and I got so angry that I left without even taking tea with her. She has no right to say things like that! She's certainly a clever talker. I held my tongue, but it really stuck in my craw to have to listen to it all without being able to say a word in your defense! And I went to see her with all good intentions!"

The Dragon King was furious. "What's so great about playing a koto? People will make fun of the girl for being behind the times. I'm no slouch when it comes to pulling at strings and things! Long ago, when I was serving a man in Echizen, everyone complimented me on how well I pulled threads and hoisted up well water for the fields. I even pulled at scarecrows' ropes! When I was serving a man at Yase, I pulled at horses' bridles and felled trees. In Yunoyama at Tsu I pulled a sledge, and in a lumberyard I pulled logs along with everyone else. When I had a master by the bay, I pulled in nets; when I lived by myself, I pulled string to make lampwicks and tugged at a handmill to grind my own tea. None of those things is in the least bit frivolous!

"In my youth I had a friend who was a blind minstrel, and he used to teach me to play the *biwa.*⁶ At the time I learned many pieces, but I soon forgot them. Even then, though, I was particularly fond of the battle scenes⁷ and would always practice them. I still remember those, and I'll teach her everything I know. But I don't have an instrument, so I'll have to borrow the Minister's lute to teach her. People flaunt their knowledge of *The Tale of Genji,* but I know parts of *The Tales of Heike* and can sing them anywhere. When people recite the *Genji,* I'll do the *Heike.* They won't show me up!

"When snow falls and melts down the tree limbs, how happy the crows must be . . . if only I could spend each and every season feeling as if it were the first of the new year . . . if I had a rice cake as wide as the sky, I'd gobble it up as if there were no tomorrow," she sang.[8] "Of all the men I've known, when I think of my old pal Kon'ichi, I have to cry. I learned that song from him. When you feel that strongly about someone, I guess that you can't help showing it. Yes, I confess it."

"How funny it is to think of all those people who brag about their talents! You never told anyone of this!" said the She-Devil. "Surely no one had any idea that you were the mistress of such a skill. I wondered why you were crying; well, it makes me cry too when I hear the reason."[9]

There came a time when the Minister's lady said to her husband, "I've heard that the nursemaids are teaching the girls to play the koto and the biwa, but I've not yet heard them play. There is a clear harvest moon tonight—shall we call them in to soothe you with their music?" The Minister agreed, and soon the young ladies arrived. It was decided to use the full moon as the theme for a poetry match. First the wife composed:

Nagame tsutsu	I have passed fully
aki no nakaba wa	half the fall gazing at the moon,
suginuredo	yet nothing compares with
koyoi bakari no	the moon of this evening.
tsukikage wa nashi	

The Minister composed:

Kazoenedo	Though I've not counted the nights,
hikari wa shirushi	the beams of light bear witness,
mizu no omo ni	shining a mirror on the water:
kagami o migaku	moon of an autumn night.
aki no yo no tsuki	

Then the older sister composed:

Tsukuzuku to	Full mooncake in the sky—
nagamuru kaimo	as much as I gaze
na nomi ni te	it's in name only
kuchi ni wa irazu	for I cannot eat it.
mochizuki no sora	

Everyone was horrified at this verse, but the Minister chuckled in amusement, commenting, "Truly, in name only . . . !" They all breathed a sigh of relief.

Presently, the musicians tuned their flutes and other instruments, and the company was treated to delightful music. Late at night, when the hearts of all were serene, the younger sister played the koto so charmingly that the Minister and his lady found it moving beyond compare. Touched to the point of tears, they commented admiringly, "No matter how wonderful music of old may have been, this is truly exceptional!"

With an air of embarrassment, the elder sister adjusted her lute in a horizontal position but did not so much as touch it. The Dragon King gritted her teeth and went forward to attend her.

"Isn't the young lady learning this instrument?" asked the Minister. "Just have her play something—anything at all." So the girl tightened the pegs, tuned the strings, grasped the plectrum, and strummed. The flute players listened intently to hear what she would play, but found nothing recognizable in the strange noises that emerged. It appeared that she was not actually playing anything at all, and everyone sat gasping. While the Minister had not expected much prowess, this was so awful that his ire was aroused.

"You play in the style of a blind minstrel," he announced. "This once referred to Semimaru, the fourth son of the Engi Emperor, abandoned by imperial decree on Ausaka Mountain, who consoled himself throughout the long years by playing the lute in his shabby hut.[10] The music of this classical lute tradition is of the past; now ways have changed. Someone based a tale on the Genpei wars, and it came to be sung by blind minstrels, who accompanied their recitations with rhythmic strumming on their lutes. This kind of strumming has nothing to do with elegant music! Did you think that all stringed instruments were the same?[11] You say that you are playing *The Tale of Genji,* but you treat it as if it were *The Tales of Heike!* This will never do! The Minamoto are the Genji; the Taira are the Heike!

"There are various explanations of the origins of *The Tale of Genji.* It is written that Princess Senshi, daughter of Emperor Murakami, and Shōshi, consort of Emperor Ichijō, wanted something to help them alleviate the tedium of their idle spring days. They desired a suitable tale to read, so they called in Murasaki Shikibu, daughter of the Governor of Echizen, and asked her if she knew of such a tale. When she explained that narratives of old were antiquated and tedious and that they had no recourse but to commission a new one, they directed her to write a tale. She secluded herself at Ishiyama Temple and wrote the fifty-four chapters of *The Tale of Genji.* Because the best chapter of all was the "Murasaki" chapter, the author came to be known as Murasaki Shikibu. You certainly have been subjected to some unfounded musical instruction![12] Did your nursemaid teach you this?" he inquired.[13]

"Just as I played it," she replied.

"Then that nursemaid is a very bad influence on you," he said. He ordered the Dragon King to resign her post and installed a far more appropriate replacement. The daughter was extremely noble, but her nurse's tutelage had made her the way she was.

It came to pass that the nurse of the younger sister fell ill unexpectedly and was obliged to take long leaves home. Knowing that she had but a short time left in this world, she wrote out a letter and sent it to her charge. It read as follows:

> I thought to conceal my own sorrows and remain by your side until you were of an age to discern the good and evil of all things for yourself, but everything here today in this unstable world vanishes on the morrow. I was concerned that you would miss me and mourn my passing; this would be terribly sad for you. By the time a woman reaches her thirties, her good manners are thoroughly ingrained; in her twenties, she tends to be unstable in all things. You, however,

are wise and discreet beyond your years. My death may be hard to bear, but you are sufficiently mature to read this advice. I am leaving everything to my brush and writing down my advice in detail. Read this for consolation when you miss me or when you have empty time on your hands.

The heart is a person's most important feature. A woman may be beautiful or accomplished, but, if her heart is inconstant, all her attractions are meaningless.[14] Be true to yourself. If imperial regard for you is great, naturally you will be the target of gossip, so do not behave in such a way as to invite censure.

One should be mature beyond her years, so, while you are young, take care to keep company with your seniors. Do not remain aloof, but keep pace with others. No matter how disagreeable something may be, you must not allow yourself to lose your temper.

A fine hand is one of a lady's greatest accomplishments: her breeding and inner intentions may be readily discerned from the faintest of brushstrokes. This illustrious imperial reign is likely to continue ever long, and there may come a time when His Majesty will view traces of your writing and be moved to praise it. As a rule, ladies should not write Chinese characters at length, but it would not be overly conspicuous if they were used only in poem prefaces or random jottings.

Drawing should not be a major accomplishment, but do try to draw people's forms beautifully and to amuse yourself with illustrated tales when you have some idle hours. Over and over I say, immerse yourself in poetry. A woman should not write ostentatious poetry, and, should she develop affection for a charming man, she should not send him superficial verse. The gist of a poem should be as fine and distinct as a crane at dusk. Learn well the poetry of the *Kokinshū* and the *Shinkokinshū*.[15]

Many things will move your heart as the years pass. In sadness and adversity, place your deepest faith in the gods and buddhas. When the gods are present, can there be any evil? Read the marvelous tales of Genji, Sagoromo, and Ise at least once, for they contain passages that are moving beyond compare. If you learn them now, you will never forget them.

Do not indulge in idle flirtation. People of taste do not exchange empty frivolous letters. Like a flower, a person in love blooms once; if you see your beloved too repeatedly, the blossom will wither. Be neither too distant nor too intimate in your relations. If you establish relations with a man lacking family connections, you will be regarded in the same light as is he, and that would be a pity. On the other hand, do not be overly distant with a suitor of quality. Let your love be as pure as newfallen snow and your ties as close as the two halves of the Kamo shrine. Keep your demeanor placid and remain calmly within the confines of your screen. Do not be too assertive when you entertain him, for nothing is as difficult as melting a man's heart.

Obey your parents' wishes as long as you live, and do not speak of odd or ugly things. Follow appropriate models of deportment, but do not attempt to tell others how they ought to behave, or you will be hated.

It is the way of this uncertain world that the pine on which one has depended withers and the needles on the lower branches scatter and disappear. After I leave this world of sadness, there will be few people remaining for you to rely on. Please remember that you cannot hide what those who serve you see and hear. Your status is such that your future is assured; in order that you gracefully learn your role, I have taken sole charge of your upbringing. I have piled up layers of quilts that you not suffer exposure to the rough winds, only to worry that you might still feel your covers to be too scanty and become chilled as the waters of a cold spring; I've fretted that the light summer breeze stirred up by my fan might not be sufficiently cool. I've tried diligently to care for you even when I realized that the flower had already bloomed and as I rejoiced at the length of your strands of hair.[16] I've prayed night and day that someone would assume the task of serving you, but I have decided to leave things to the workings of your own good karma.

Even if you live in splendid and luxurious surroundings and receive imperial favor, never cause a disturbance or be jealous. If you find yourself in unhappy straits, do not allow your anguish to show. Should your suffering continue, create circumstances such that you may obtain permission to leave your position. Collect your scattered, wounded feelings, become a nun, and live quietly. This advice applies not only to life at the palace. Heed this well: however you are situated, never make a fuss or assert yourself.

Though you may prosper as you would like in this world, there remains a chance that you will lose your way on the dark path in the next world. Your parents deserve your highest respect and regard. No matter how much time passes, remember always the well-loved pillar in the hall.[17] In order to maintain your bearings on that dark path to come, you must always keep that source of light firmly in sight, never deviating from your intent. Follow your parents' wishes in all things. May you never cause them to suffer sleepless nights of worry on your behalf! There are many in this world who speak ill of a person on her death. This is a terrible thing indeed. Remember that to leave a bad reputation behind you is far worse than enduring shame in your lifetime. Do not abandon those who have long stood by you. Night and day I pray that your destiny be auspicious and that people of worth invoke your example for others to follow. The gods of Kasuga never lie.[18]

I run the risk of seeming repetitive, but remember that people are judged by their conduct. Keep this in mind and observe irreproachable behavior. No matter how holy a monk may be, do not allow him near you or visit his cell very frequently, else rumors fly that he was your lover. There are many wise nuns in this world; attach yourself to one and rely on her as your preceptress of the world to come.

Proper blending of incense requires great sensitivity. Should you present some to another, be certain that the fragrance is well prepared. A person's inner heart may be known through her fragrance; take care that yours is extremely beautiful. Fans also tell much about a woman, so hold yours in such a way that it reflects your inner modesty.

While the blossoms of spring and maples of fall are not undeserving of the attention they command, allow yourself to regard the withered frosty landscape as well, for nothing is more deeply moving than a desolate winter field. Cultivate a garden and watch it grow; through it may be understood the ways of this evanescent world. You must never be arrogant. Though a weed may be ripped up and discarded, the root endures, but will eventually die with diligent trimming. If you vigilently dispel dishonest or wild impulses, they will cease to spring up.

Both sadness and happiness are but a dream. Think well on this and be discerning. If things do not go your way, never harbor a shred of hatred for anyone, and place your welfare in the hands of the gods and buddhas. Regard your elders as your parents and your juniors as your sisters, and treat all with kindness. Comport yourself correctly, and do not assert your own will. Be kind to others, and always have compassion.

The younger sister missed her dear nurse all the more whenever she read this letter, and she carried it with her at all times. The Dragon King heard of it and said to herself, "So, she's been up to her usual smug drivel again! I can beat that!" And not to be outdone, she wrote her own missive:

I planned never to leave you, but, because of certain ill-intentioned people and their slander, I've been tossed out for being too strong willed. This is what they mean when they speak about golden words falling on tin ears.

First of all, people are how they behave. It's no good to be quiet and distant to others. Just come right up to their back door and run in to chat with them. People will call you perverse if you don't talk with them. Speak freely like a mockingbird, and let fly words about all you know and don't know. Treat everyone with the familiarity between a parent and a child, no matter from what distant country or unknown village they may hail. That way, you'll be praised for your open nature. If you're too honest about your inner feelings, however, you'll look like a foolish country bumpkin, so it's better to tell falsehoods and fabrications.

If you're too shy, people will make fun of you and call you a despicable weakling, but, if you always act as if you're angry, they'll take you seriously. It's bad not to have desires. If you want something, grab it, even if it belongs to another. They may not give it to you, but that's no skin off your back, and, if only one in ten gives you something, you'll still be ahead of the game.

As long as we live in this sad world, we must eat. No matter whom you marry, the way things begin sets the tone for what follows. Therefore, if your servings are too small and you want for anything, just complain bitterly and tell them that you are not used to such conditions. You must be greedy. Eating is very important, and eating sparsely makes you look pretentious. Even if there's just a smidgeon of room left in your stomach, shovel it down in big gulps. This is particularly true of wine, which won't hurt you no matter how much you drink. And, when you're drunk, say just what you please. Drink it all straight down the hatch! Besides, it's fun to watch people when they're drunk.

They say that it's bad to lose your temper in front of your husband, but that's not so. If he's worth being with and there's something that makes you angry, become a vengeful harpy, just like in the nō play *Kanawa*.[19] Let your words pour out, and show your fearsome heart.

Let neither parent nor child impede you—it is enough that you alone fare well. The quest for the life to come is the quickest path to poverty. Devote all your prayers to wealth and benefit in this life.

It is amusing to compare the hearts of these two nursemaids through their letters. With small children, everything depends on upbringing, for they do good and evil just as they are taught. Even in play they imitate and listen to their betters. Take the beast called the monkey, who lives far from human habitation: if you care for him and teach him tricks, he will do just as you have instructed. Moreover, humans can learn anything at all. A person's lack of accomplishments, manners, or a pleasant disposition is solely the fault of the parent. One can well understand the anguish of parents who wonder how they could have raised such a dreadful child. One must make children recognize good and evil.

Eventually the younger sister entered service in the palace and became an attendant to the Empress, where she remained pure and open in heart. A high-ranking lord fell in love with her, and she became an example for all people of good breeding. The older sister was by nature noble and able to distinguish good from evil, and so she grew up without flaws. Later, she became the wife of the Minister of the Center and, it is said, was also upheld as an example of fortunate destiny.[20]

NOTES

1. For a brief biography of Abutsu and translation of her most famous work, the *Izayoi nikki* (rendered as *The Diary of the Waning Moon*), see Edwin O. Reischauer and Joseph K. Yamagiwa, *Translations from Early Japanese Literature,* Harvard Yenching Studies 29 (Cambridge, Mass.: Harvard University Press, 1972).

2. Two highly regarded classic court romances.

3. The nurse's spoken line is a vestigial caption.

4. This passage from "Look here . . ." until ". . . just to think about it" is a vestigial caption.

5. This exchange, beginning with "Now, play this . . ." through ". . . What a pity!" is a vestigial caption.

6. *Biwa* usually translates as "lute," although the term refers to several different kinds of instruments.

7. Blind itinerant minstrels used a particular kind of lute *(mōsō biwa)* to accompany their recitation of the war epic *The Tales of the Heike.* As will soon be obvious, the Dragon King knows only this kind of instrument, which is quite different from the biwa used in courtly music making.

8. This is probably an intentionally garbled rendition of a contemporary song.

9. The dialogue from "When snow falls . . ." to ". . . when I hear the reason" is another caption-like passage.

10. For a study of this semilegendary blind lute player, see Susan Matisoff, *The Legend of Semimaru, Blind Musician of Japan* (New York: Columbia University Press, 1978).

11. "Kotobiwa to mōseba onaji koto no yō ni kokoroekeru ni ya." This line is problematic within its context; the translation is mostly guesswork.

12. This is a wild guess at an extremely cryptic line: "kotobiwa to iitsuzukemu to te yoshinaki towazugatari shi haberinu." *Kotobiwa* appears earlier in the text. It may refer to the koto and biwa, stringed instruments, music, or the arts in general. Alternatively, the latter part of the line may refer to Murasaki Shikibu, putative author of *The Tale of Genji*, and the "unfounded confessions" *(yoshinaki towazugatari)* would be that novel. Medieval Buddhist thinking held that Murasaki Shikibu suffered in hell for having written fiction.

13. The Minister is pointing out fundamental mistakes the girl has made. First, recitation of *The Tales of Heike* to a biwa accompaniment was limited to blind male minstrels and was hardly a seemly art for a young lady of nobility. The biwa used in such performances, called a *heike biwa,* was different than that used in courtly music. Second, to my knowlege, *The Tale of Genji* was never played to musical accompaniment, least of all to a heike biwa, which was played more for rhythmic than melodic effect. Finally, the girl seems to have conflated the two tales in her performance. Knowledge of *The Tale of Genji* was considered essential to any young woman's upbringing.

14. The same statement is made in the ending of *A Discretionary Tale;* perhaps it was a contemporary saying.

15. The two most famous imperial poetry anthologies.

16. A noblewoman's hair was never cut; the older she became, the longer her hair grew.

17. Probably a reference to the "Makibashira" chapter of *The Tale of Genji,* in which a girl, loathe to depart her home, leaves behind a poem on a pillar.

18. This line is unclear within this context. The *Niwa no oshie,* from which this letter is derived, mentions that the gods of Kasuga Shrine had predicted that the girl would receive great honors at court.

19. Based on a story about a jealous woman turning into a fiend and exacting revenge on her rival. Also recounted in *The Tale of the Brazier.*

20. The text seems to contradict itself in saying that the girl's innate nobility compensated for her poor upbringing, but the author must have felt it necessary to end the story on a happy, felicitous note.

Lazy Tarō
Monogusa Tarō

Few otogi-zōshi have inspired such a variety of interpretations and reactions as has *Lazy Tarō*, a whimsical account of a lazy country bumpkin who reveals a surprising talent for witty verbal repartee. The endearingly oafish Tarō has been hailed as an exemplar of the fresh spirit of the late medieval period, as a heroic god in the syncretic Shinto-Buddhist pantheon, as a contemporary peasant hero, and even as an entirely new character type on the stage of Japanese narrative literature: the self-made man unashamed of his humble origins.[1] No matter how one interprets Tarō and his story, for sheer entertainment value it ranks as one of the most popular of all otogi-zōshi.

The basic plot of *Lazy Tarō* was most probably derived from *The Little Man* or its variants. Where the little man is a pathetically appealing, self-conscious gentleman, however, Tarō is a fractious, insouciant, and unkempt maverick who does exactly as he likes no matter what the consequences. In many respects, *Lazy Tarō* resembles the medieval Japanese theatrical farce, kyōgen; indeed, the wife-snaring scene at Kiyomizu Temple has much in common with the kyōgen play *Nikujūhachi*. Like kyōgen, the story of *Lazy Tarō* contains numerous puns and riddles, reflecting the delight contemporary Japanese took in verbal humor. Tarō's ready wit, unprepossessing appearance, and buffoonery bring to mind that delightful kyōgen stock character Tarō kaja, the servant who always manages to outwit his betters.

This translation is based on the Shibukawa Seiemon illustrated block printed booklet set in the Ueno Library, Tokyo, printed with annotations in *Otogi-zōshi* (pp. 187–207). Illustrations have been provided through the kindness of the Tokyo University Library. An earlier version of this translation appeared in *Monumenta Nipponica* 44:2 (Summer 1989).

At the furthest reaches of the Tōsen route,[2] in a place called Atarashi village, in Tsukama, one of the ten districts of Shinano Province, lived a peculiar man called Lazy Tarō Hijikasu,[3] so dubbed because no one in the province could equal him in sheer laziness. He may have been called lazy, but he had a wonderful idea for building a house. He would construct a clay enclosure with a gate in three of the four sides. Inside, to the north, south, east, and west, he would create ponds and islands planted with pines and cedars. Arched bridges, their pillars crowned in shining ornamentation, would link the islands to the garden. It was truly a marvelous plan! There would be a retainers' quarters twelve ken[4] wide, connecting corridors nine ken long, a water-viewing pavilion, galleries, and plum, pawlonia, and bamboo courtyards abloom with myriad varieties of flowers. There would be a main chamber of twelve ken, roofed in cypress bark, with damask-covered ceilings, gold- and silver-studded beam ends and rafters, and splendid woven hanging blinds. Everything would be magnificent, right down to the stables and servants' quarters. If only he could build such a fine mansion! But he utterly lacked the means, and so he was obliged to make do with a straw mat upheld by four bamboo poles—a most uncomfortable residence in either rain or shine. As if the lean-to wasn't wretched enough, Tarō had more than his due share of chilblains, fleas, lice, and even elbow grime. He had no assets, so he couldn't set up shop; he tilled no land, so he had no food. For days on end he would lie there without rising once.

On one occasion, a kind soul said to him, "Here, take this, you must be hungry," and gave him five rice cakes left over from a wedding feast. Tarō received food so rarely that he immediately devoured four of them. As for the last, however, if he kept it and didn't eat it, he could rely on it later; if he ate it now and left nothing, his stomach might be full, but then he could not expect more later. Just looking at that rice cake provided a certain solace, so he decided to keep it until he received something else. Lazy Tarō would lie there playing with it, rolling it around on his chest, polishing it with oil blotted from his nose, wetting it with spit, and balancing it on his head. While he was thus amusing himself, the rice cake slipped from his grasp and rolled over to the side of the road. Tarō looked at it and pondered. He was too lazy to get up and retrieve it. Figuring that sooner or later someone was bound to come by, he waited for three days, waving around a bamboo stick to ward off the dogs and crows who came to nibble at it, but not one person came along.

Finally, on the third day, there came the awaited passerby, none other than the local Land Steward, Saemon no jō Nobuyori, off on an autumn hunting expedition accompanied by a host of some fifty to sixty mounted retainers carrying white-eyed falcons. When Tarō spotted him, he craned his neck and called, "Hey you! Excuse me, but there's a rice cake over there. Would you mind fetching it for me?"

But Nobuyori paid no heed and continued on his way.

"How in the world can such a lazy man possibly manage an entire domain?" thought Tarō. "It isn't that much trouble to get down and pick up a rice cake. I thought I was the only lazy fellow around, but there must be many of us."

"What a heartless lord!" he grumbled aloud, quite provoked.

Had Nobuyori been a short-tempered man, he would have taken offense, and there is no telling what he might have done. But

instead he reined in his horse and asked his retainer, "Is that fellow the notorious Lazy Tarō?"

"There couldn't possibly be two of them, sir. That must be him."

"You there, how do you make a living?" asked Nobuyori directly.

"When people give me something, I'll eat anything at all. When they don't, I go without for four, five, as many as ten days."

"What a sorry plight! You must do something to help yourself! There is a saying that those who rest under the shade of the same tree and who drink of the same water share a karmic connection from a former life. That of all places in the world you were born into my domain must mean there is a bond between us. Cultivate some land and live off that."

"But I have no land."

"Then I'll give you some."

"I'm too lazy—I don't want to work."

"Then set up a shop."

"I have nothing to sell."

"Then I'll give you something."

"It's hard to do something you're not used to, and I've never done it before."

"What an odd fellow!" thought Nobuyori. "I must do something to help him out." Pulling out an inkstone, he wrote the following edict and had it distributed throughout his lands:

Lazy Tarō is to be fed daily: three measures of rice twice a day and wine once a day. Those who fail to comply will be expelled from this domain.

Everyone thought this a prime example of the saying, "The unreasonableness of a lord's decree," but for three years they fed Tarō as ordered.

At the end of spring of the third year, Arisue, Governor of Shinano and Major Counselor of Nijō, ordered the village of Atarashi to supply a laborer to work in the capital. All the villagers gathered together to decide which household should provide the laborer. It had been such a long time since this sort of demand had been imposed that they were at a loss about what to do.

Then someone suggested, "How about sending Lazy Tarō?"

Another objected, "That's ridiculous! He's so lazy he wouldn't even pick up a rice cake lying in the road—he waited for the Steward to pass by and asked *him* to get it!"

"Convincing someone like Tarō to do it just might be the answer. Come on, let's give it a try," said another. So four or five elders got together and went to Taro's hovel.

"Hey there, Lord Lazy Bones! Please help us out! It's our turn to send a man for public labor."

"What's that?" asked Tarō.

"We have to find a laborer—sort of like a longshoreman."

"How long is that? It must be awfully big!"⁵

"No, no! It's nothing like that! A laborer is someone we send from among the villagers to go serve in the capital. You should go out of gratitude to us for having fed you for three years."

"That's not something you cooked up yourselves, is it? I'll bet the Steward put you up to this." Tarō was not at all inclined to go.

"Look at it this way: it's for your own good," said one of them. "I mean, a fellow becomes a man when he takes a wife, and a girl becomes a woman when she has a husband. So, rather than live all alone in this broken-down shack, why don't you start making plans to be a responsible adult? You know, they say that there are three times in a man's life when he comes into his own: when he first wears adult trousers, when he holds a job, and when he takes a wife. And you grow up even more when you travel. Country folks have no sense of human warmth, but city folks do. In the capital, no one is despised, and fine-looking people will live with anyone as husband and wife. So why don't you take off to the capital, get together with a woman who suits your fancy, and make a man of yourself?" he urged, presenting a fine array of arguments.

"Fine with me! If that's the case, then please send me there as soon as possible!" said Lazy Tarō. He was ready to depart immediately. The delighted villagers got together some traveling money and sent him off.

Lazy Tarō went along the Tōsen road, and, as he passed through each successive way station, he showed not a trace of laziness. On the seventh day, he arrived in the capital. "I'm the laborer come from Shinano," he announced proudly.

Everyone stared at him and laughed. "Can such a grimy, filthy creature possibly exist in this world?" they snickered among themselves. But the Major Counselor took him on. "It matters not how he looks," he said. "As long as he's a hard worker, he'll be fine."

Kyoto far surpassed anything Tarō had ever seen in Shinano. The mountains to the east and west, the palaces, temples, and shrines —everything was endlessly fascinating. Tarō was not lazy in the least; indeed, never had there been a more diligent worker than he. They kept him seven months, although he was obliged to serve only three. Finally, in the eleventh month, he was released from duty and decided to return home.

Tarō went to his lodgings to contemplate his situation. He had been told to bring back a good wife; the prospect of returning home all alone was too bleak. Wondering how he might find a wife, he approached his landlord for advice.

"I'm going back to Shinano. If you can, would you please find a woman willing to be the wife of a man like me?"

The landlord laughed and thought to himself, "I'd like to see any woman who would marry the likes of you!" But aloud he replied, "It's easy enough to ask around and find a woman, but marriage is quite another matter. What you really want is a streetwalker."

"What's a streetwalker? What do you mean by that?"

"Someone without a husband, who meets you for money— that's a streetwalker."

"Well, then, please find one for me. I have some money for my trip, some twelve or thirteen *mon*. Please use it for her."

The landlord thought that he had never met a bigger fool. "If you want one, you'll have to go out and cruise around."[6]

"Cruise around? What's that supposed to mean?"

"That's when you look at all the women who don't have men with them and who aren't riding in carriages, and then you pick out a nice-looking one who catches your fancy. It's all right—you're allowed to do it."

"If that's the case, then I'll give it a try."

Tarō set out to try his luck at Kiyomizu Temple on the eighteenth of the eleventh month,[7] just as his landlord had suggested. He was dressed in the same rags he had long worn even in Shinano: a rough hempen singlet, so ancient that the color and pattern were indistinguishable, a straw rope wrapped around his waist, a pair of old frayed scuffs[8] on his feet, and a bamboo staff in his hand. It was late in the year, and the bitter winds were so fierce that Tarō's nose ran. He looked like a sooty stupa as he waited by the main gate, standing rigidly with his arms outstretched. The returning worshipers thought him a frightful sight. Whatever could he be waiting for? All took care to avoid him, and not a single person ventured near. Groups of women ranging in age from seventeen to twenty surged by, but not one spared him a glance. Thousands of people must have passed as he stood there vacillating from dawn to dusk, rejecting one woman after another.

Then a young lady emerged. She might have been seventeen or eighteen years old, a veritable blossom of spring. With her raven locks and lovely midnight blue eyebrows, she looked just like a mountain cherry in bloom. Her sidelocks curved as gracefully as the

wings of an autumn cicada; she was blessed with the beauty of the myriad marks of the angels and was as radiant as a Golden Buddha. Her charm extended from her arching eyebrows right down to the hem of her robes, which danced with every step she took. She wore a crimson skirt over her gayly colored robe and light, unlined sandals on her feet. The scent of plum blossoms rose from her hair, which was longer than she was tall. She had come to worship at the temple, accompanied by a maidservant almost as pretty as she was. To Lazy Tarō, here indeed had come his bride. He waited eagerly, arms outstretched, ready to embrace and kiss her. The lady caught sight of him and leaned over to her maid.

"What's that?" she asked.

"It's a person," came the reply.

"How dreadful! How can I avoid him?" she thought in a panic, hastily taking another path.

"Oh, no!" thought Tarō. "She's heading that way! I have to catch up with her!" He went up to her with open arms and poked his dirty head under her lovely sedge hat. Bringing his face up to hers, he cried, "Hey, lady!" and threw his arms around her. Taken by surprise, she was speechless with confusion. People in the bustling crowd cried out, "How terrible! Isn't it frightful?" but everyone was careful to give them a wide berth.

Tarō held on tightly. "Hey, lady! It's been a long time! I've seen you all over the place—at Ōhara, Seryū and Shizuhara, Kōdō, Kawasaki, and Nakayama, Chōrakuji, Kiyomizu, Rokuhara, and Rokkakudō, Hōrinji, Saga, Daigo, Uzumasa, Kobata, Kurusu, Yahata, Yodo, Kuramadera, Sumiyoshi, the Gojō Tenjin, the Kibune Myōjin, the Hiyoshi Sannō, Kitano, Gion, Kasuga, Kamo[9]—what do you think? Huh? Huh?"

At this, the lady decided that he was just another country bumpkin whose landlord had told him to go out cruising around. She could outwit someone like that.

"Is that so?" she said coolly. "There are so many people looking on now; why don't you come visit me at my home?"

"Where do you live?" he asked.

The lady assumed that she could confuse him with some fancy

phrases and make her escape while he was puzzling them out. "I live in a place called Underpine," she replied.

"Oh, I see. Under a pine torch is bright, so you must live at Brightstone Bay."[10]

She was taken aback. Well, he might understand that, but he certainly wouldn't be able to guess another. "It's in a village where the sun sets."

"Ah, a village where the sun sets. I can guess that one, too. It must be deep in Dark Mountain.[11] Whereabouts?"

"That indeed is my home. You must look for Lampwick Lane."

"Tallow Lane?[12] Whereabouts?"

"That indeed is my home. It is a shy village."

"Hidden Village?[13] Whereabouts?"

"That indeed is my home. It is a village of cloaks."

"Brocade Lane?[14] Whereabouts?"

"That indeed is my home. It is in a land of solace."

"Love-Tryst Province?[15] Whereabouts?"

"At an unclouded village of cosmetics."

"Mirror Lodge?[16] Whereabouts?"

"In an autumnal land."

"Ripe-Rice Province?[17] Whereabouts?"

"That indeed is my home. It is in a land of twenty."

"Youthful Province?[18] Whereabouts?"

As long as he was responding like this, there was no way for the lady to escape. Perhaps she could recite some poetry and flee while he was working it out. Taking her cue from his bamboo stick, she recited:

Karatake o	Rather hard to join
tsue ni tsukitaru	with the man I see
mono nareba	carrying a staff
fushi soigataki	of many-jointed bamboo.[19]
hito o miru kana	

"Oh, dear!" thought Tarō. "The lady's saying that she doesn't want to sleep with me." And he replied:

Yorozu yo no	Each and every stalk is
take no yo goto ni	nightly linked together.
sou fushi no	Why, then, can there be no joining
nado karatake ni	with this bamboo bough?[20]
fushi nakaru beki	

"Oh, no!" thought the lady. "This man is saying that he wants to sleep with me! But his poetic sensitivity does make him much more refined than he looks." And she said:

Hanase kashi	Loosen your net!
ami no itome no	The eyes are fixed too tightly.
shigekereba	Release your hand,
kono te o hanare	then we shall speak.[21]
mono katari sen	

Tarō understood that she was asking him to let her go and wondered what to do. So he responded:

Nani ga kono	So what if the network
ami no itome wa	of eyes is fixed on you?
shigeku to mo	Let me kiss you,
kuchi o suwaseyo	then my hand will loosen.
te o ba yurusan	

At this, the lady realized that poetic repartee was getting her nowhere. And so she recited:

Omou nara	If you love me,
toite mo kimase	then call on me.
waga yado wa	Mine is the house
karatachibana no	with the orange-blossom gate.[22]
murasaki no kado	

As Tarō took note of her words, he gradually allowed his grip to relax. She shook herself free and dashed off, leaving her sedge hat, cloak, sandals, and servant behind. Tarō was devastated at the disappearance of his lady love. He grabbed his staff, called out, "Lady, where are you going?" and took off in pursuit.

The lady was familiar with the streets, and, sure that this was her last chance, made her getaway by crisscrossing back and forth, through this alley and around that corner, like a cherry petal scattering in the spring wind.

"Hey, where are you going, sweetie?" Tarō called out again. He headed down an alley so as to meet up with her at the next corner, but somehow lost track of her. Retracing his steps, he found nothing, and passersby all denied having seen her. Finally, he returned to his post at Kiyomizu. "Now," he told himself, "she was standing facing this way, then she turned that way, said such and such . . . oh, wherever did she go?"

His burning love seemed to be hopeless until he suddenly remembered that she had spoken of an orange-blossom gate. He would have to find out where that was. So he wrapped a piece of paper around his stick and went into a soldiers' guard post.[23]

"I'm up from the country and have forgotten an address. It's a place called Orange-Blossom Gate, or something like that. Where might that be?"

"Seems that there's a place by that name back of Seventh Avenue, at the residence of the Lord Governor of Buzen. Go down this lane and ask there," he was told.

And indeed it was the place. Tarō felt as if he had already found his lady, and he was filled with joy. Here people were absorbed in all sorts of amusements: polo, chess, *sugoroku,* music, and song. Tarō searched everywhere in vain for his beloved. Hoping that she might yet emerge, he concealed himself beneath a veranda and waited.

Here, the lady was known as Jijū no Tsubone.[24] Late that night, she returned to her quarters after serving at the Governor's court. She stood in the outer corridor and called to her maid, Nadeshiko.

"Hasn't the moon risen yet? I wonder what happened to that man from Kiyomizu? If it had been this dark when I ran into him, it would have been the end of me."

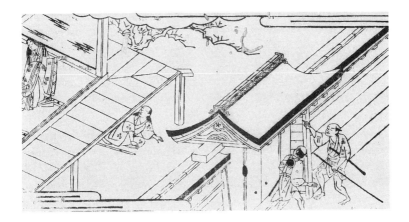

"How detestable he was!" replied Nadeshiko. "He couldn't possibly come here! But do be careful—speak of the devil, and he's sure to appear, you know!"[25]

Lazy Tarō was listening from under the veranda. Here was his bride! In his joy that their bond had not been severed, he pranced out and leaped up beside her. "Hey, lady! I've been pretty worried about you, sweetie! Darned near broke my neck trying to find you!"

The lady was utterly aghast. She scrambled behind her screen to escape and remained there in a state of shock, her face as vacant as the sky above. Presently, she moaned to her maid, "How dreadfully tenacious he is! He's actually here! Of all the men in the world, that such a dirty, disgusting creature should fall in love with me! How awful!"

Just then a company of watchmen came by. "Have you seen a stranger around?" they asked. "The dogs are in an uproar!"

"Oh, no!" she thought, "What if they kill him? As a woman, my sins are already deep enough, what with the Five Hindrances and Three Duties."[26] She wept bitter tears. What harm could there be in putting him up for the night, then slipping him out at dawn? She told the maid to put out an old mat for him to sit on. So the maid went to Tarō and informed him that he could remain until dawn, when he must leave quietly, taking care that no one saw him. She

spread out a mat trimmed with elaborately patterned edging, the likes of which Tarō had never seen, and bade him sit on it.

Lazy Tarō was quite exhausted from all the running around he had done that day. He hoped that they would bring him something —anything—soon. What might it be? If it were chestnuts, he would first roast, then eat them; if persimmons, pears, or rice cakes, he would gobble them down right away. If they gave him wine, he would drink almost twenty cups of it. As he was sitting there musing expectantly, the maid brought out a knife, salt, and a rough-edged basket filled with chestnuts, persimmons, and pears.

"Darn it," said Tarō to himself. "In spite of her fine looks, she's treating me like a horse or an ox, giving me this fruit all jumbled together in a basket without setting it out nicely on a lid[27] or paper. It's too much! There must be something more to it. Let's see: she gave me the fruit all together, so that must mean that she wants to get together with me. And the chestnuts mean that she won't repeat the nutty things she said before,[28] the pears that she wishes to be paired only with me.[29] But what about the persimmons and salt? Well, I can use them together in a poem:

Tsu no kuni no   Since this is the fruit
Naniwa no ura no   of Naniwa Bay in Tsu,
kaki nareba   it has crossed no seas
umi wataranedo   but is well pickled in salt.[30]
shio wa tsukikeri

The lady overheard this and marveled at his exceptional sensitivity. Here indeed was an example of the proverbial "lotus blooming from the mire" and "gold wrapped in straw." "Here, take this," she said, passing him some ten sheets of paper. Tarō wondered at this, but concluded that, although she had written no message, she must want him to write a response. And so he composed:

Chihayaburu	You give me mighty divine paper
kami o tsukai ni	for my use.
tabitaru wa	Could this mean that
ware o yashiro to	you think me a sacred shrine?[31]
omou ka ya kimi	

"I can't hold out any longer!" she cried. "Bring him in!" She gathered together a pair of wide trousers, a robe, a court hat, and a sword for him to wear.

Delighted at this happy turn of events, Tarō Hijikasu wrapped his old hand-me-downs around his staff. She probably meant to lend him the new attire just for the night, and he would need his old rags again in the morning.

"Dogs, don't you dare eat these! Thieves, don't you dare steal these!" he thought, tossing the bundle under the veranda. Then, confronted with the problem of putting on the trousers and robe, he looped the ties around his neck and draped the pants over his shoulders, such that the maid was obliged to help him out of his predicament. As she was about to put the court hat on his head, she saw that his hair was such a tangle of dirt, fleas, and lice that it looked as if it had never known a comb. But somehow she managed to put it to rights, perched the hat on his head, and led him inside.

Tarō had been able to navigate the mountains and cliffs of Shinano, but never before had he encountered such a slippery smooth surface as these oiled floor boards, and he skidded and slipped to and fro as he walked. Nadeshiko led him behind the lady's screen and disappeared. Just as he was about to approach her, he lost his footing, tumbled head over heels, and landed squarely on top of her cherished koto, Tehikimaru, smashing it to smithereens. The lady was heartsick. Tears streaming down a face turned as red as the leaves of autumn, she said:

> Kyō yori wa   Whatever can I do now
> waga nagusami ni   to while away my idle hours?
> nani ka sen

Gazing up at her from his prone position, Tarō returned:

> Kotowari nareba   The koto's smashed; my hopes are dashed—
> mono mo iwarezu   I'm so abashed![32]

With this, the lady realized that Tarō had the soul of a gentleman. So moved was she that they must have shared a karmic bond, for this could not be the shallow connection of a single lifetime. She pledged herself to him.

Dawn broke all too soon, and, as Tarō was making ready for a hasty departure, she said, "I was moved in spite of myself to invite you in. Surely this means that we share a bond from a former life. If you hold me dear to your heart, please remain here. I may be a court lady, but what difference does that make?" And so Tarō agreed to stay.

Together the lady and her maid worked day and night setting him to rights. They had him bathe every day for a week, and by the seventh day he sparkled like a jewel. Each successive day thereafter he shone more brilliantly and came to acquire a reputation as a handsome man and an accomplished poet of linked verse. As his lady was of high rank, she was able to instruct him in all matters of gentlemanly deportment. His dress was impeccable: from the hang of his trousers to the angle of his court hat and the coif of his hair, he easily outdid the highest of nobility. The Governor of Buzen heard about him and summoned him to an audience. Seeing Tarō so beautifully dressed, he remarked, "You are indeed a handsome man. What is your name?"

"Lazy Tarō."

This was so inappropriate that the Governor renamed him Uta no Saemon.[33]

Eventually, word reached the inner sanctum of the palace, and Tarō was summoned to report there at once. He tried to decline the honor, but to no avail. He rode in a carriage to the palace, and on his arrival he was ushered into the formal audience hall.

"I hear that you are a prodigy at linked verse. Compose a couple of links," ordered the Emperor. Just then, a warbler flew down, perched on a plum branch, and sang. Hearing this, Tarō recited:

Uguisu no	Is it because spring rain
nuretaru koe no	has spilled over the umbrella
kikoyuru wa	of plum blossoms that
ume no hanagasa	the warbler is bathed in tears?
moru ya harusame	

"Do they call it a plum where you come from?" asked the Emperor. Without hesitation, Tarō replied:

Shinano ni wa	In Shinano
baika to iu mo	the flower is called *baika;*
ume no hana	in the capital
miyako no koto wa	what might they call the plum?
ikaga aruran	

The Emperor was very impressed. "Who are your ancestors?" he asked.

"I have no ancestors."

The Emperor ordered him to inquire of the Deputy Governor of Shinano about his ancestry. The Deputy Governor in turn gave the commission to the local steward, and eventually the results were brought to the Emperor in a missive wrapped in rush matting. On examination, the Emperor learned that the Middle Captain of the Second Rank, the second son of the fifty-third emperor, Ninmei, also known as Fukakusa,[34] had been exiled to Shinano, where he lived for many years. He had no children, and his desperation led him to make a pilgrimage to Zenkō Temple, where he petitioned the Amida Buddha. As a result, he was blessed with a son. When the child was but three years old, his parents died, and thus he dropped to a lowly status and was tainted with the dirt of humble commoners.

On reading this, the Emperor saw that Tarō was not far removed from the imperial line itself. He dubbed him the Middle Captain of Shinano and granted him the domains of Kai and Shinano. Accompanied by his wife, the Middle Captain went to the village of Asahi in Shinano. Since Nobuyori, the Steward of Atarashi, had been so kind to him, he made him General Administrator of his domains and awarded land to each of the farmers who had fed him for three years. For the site of his own mansion, he selected Tsukama, and there set up his household. Everyone, regardless of social standing, obeyed him, and he governed his domains in peace and tranquility under the protection of the gods and buddhas. He lived for 120 years, producing many descendants, and his household overflowed with the Seven Treasures and abundant wealth. He became a god of longevity and the Great Deity of Odaka,[35] while his wife was a manifestation of the Asai[36] Gongen.

This occurred during the reign of Emperor Montoku.[37] Tarō was a manifestation of a god who brought together those who had gathered karmic merit from a previous life. He vowed that, when anyone, man or woman, came to worship him, he would fulfill the request. Usually, ordinary men are provoked to anger at talk of their origins,[38] but, when the origins of a god are revealed, the torments of the Three Heats[39] are quelled, and he is immediately delighted. As revealed in this tale, even a lazy man may be pure and sincere at heart.[40]

The god has vowed that those who daily read this story or tell it to others will be filled with riches and achieve their hearts' desires. How wonderfully blessed!

NOTES

1. For a discussion of *Lazy Tarō* as a transformation of the Buddhist *honjimono* tale tradition, see Virginia Skord, "From Rags to Riches and Beyond: Monogusa Tarō," *Monumenta Nipponica* 44:2 (1989).
2. One of the eight old travel routes. Shinano corresponds to present-day Nagano Prefecture.

3. Hijikasu may represent a combination of *hiji* (dirt) and *kasu* (dregs). Now a common personal name for an eldest male child, Tarō signifies the first and best among many. Thus, his name could be interpreted as designating the most eminently filthy.

4. A ken was approximately 1.8 meters in length.

5. Tarō assumes that the *naga* (long) of *nagabu* (long-term laborer) refers to a long object. I have tried to preserve the flavor of the original by using "longshoreman," although of course this does not appear in the text.

6. *Tsujidori*, lit., "street-corner picking," or soliciting a prostitute.

7. A fixed festival day at Kiyomizu Temple, an extremely popular trysting site that houses the Tsuma Kannon, a Buddhist deity thought to provide a wife for a single man and, by extension, a mate for any supplicant. The dwarf of *The Little Man* works nearby and prays here.

8. *Monogusa zōri* (lit., "lazy sandals"), straw sandals without heels used by foot soldiers and priests for their light weight and ease of wearing. It stands to reason that Lazy Tarō should wear lazy footgear.

9. This passage comprises a listing of famous sites in and around Kyoto.

10. "Underpine," *matsu no moto*. "Brightstone Bay," *Akashi no ura*. In this and the subsequent riddles, the places that Tarō correctly identifies are actual place names, translated in such a way as to preserve the point of the riddles.

11. A village where the sun sets *(higureru sato)* would be dark, so it must lie in the depths of Dark Mountain *(Kurama no oku)*.

12. Because lamps are lit with tallow, "Lampwick Lane" *(tomoshibi no kōji)* indicates "Tallow Lane" *(Abura no kōji)*.

13. A shy village *(hazukashi no sato)* would be hidden from sight, hence "Hidden Village" *(Shinobu no sato)*.

14. Vestments are linked with fabrics: a village of cloaks *(uwagi no sato)* indicates Brocade Lane *(Nishiki no kōji)*.

15. Meeting a lover brings solace; a land of solace *(nagusamu kuni)* would be in Love-Tryst Province *(Ōmi no kuni)*.

16. The unclouded village of cosmetics *(keshō suru kumori naki sato)* indicates a mirror, which is always clear and used in applying cosmetics, linked to Mirror Lodge *(Kagami no shuku)*.

17. In an autumnal land *(aki suru kuni)*, the rice would be ripened and ready for harvest, so it must refer to Ripe-Rice Province *(Inaba no kuni)*.

18. Twenty is a youthful age, so a land of twenty *(hatachi no kuni)* refers to Youthful Province *(Wakasa no kuni)*.

19. The verse puns on *fushi*, "lie down" and "bamboo joint."

20. This verse incorporates the pun of the preceding poem and extends it with puns on *yo*, "world," "stalk," and "night."

21. This puns on *itome*, "eyes" of a net, and *hitome*, "eyes of others."

22. The last two lines of her response are unclear. *Karatachibana* refers to the Chinese orange blossom, which has either a reddish or a white hue. *Murasaki* is lavender. Here, *murasaki* may refer to *murasaki sō*, a small plant with white blossoms similar to the Chinese orange blossom. On the other hand, the gate simply may be planted with both types of flowers.

23. Tying paper to a stick may have been a medieval practice demonstrating humility to an unknown person.

24. It was common for high-ranking women to be referred to by the offices of a male relative. *Jijū*, "chamberlain," is of middling-high rank; *tsubone* was a respectful term for aristocratic women.

25. I have borrowed an English-language expression for a similar Japanese saying to the effect that, if you speak of someone, he is sure to show up.

26. See the text and n. 7 to *The Tale of the Brazier*. Both principles were commonly invoked in medieval literature to express the innate sinfulness and inferiority of women.

27. Lids were used as trays.

28. This involves a pun on *kuri*, "chestnut," and *kurigoto*, "repetition." The line has been translated to create a slightly different pun.

29. A pun on *nashi*, "pear" and "none."

30. This puns on *kaki*, "persimmon" and "oyster," and *umiwataru*, "ripen" and "cross the sea." Tsu, an old name for Settsu, is in the Osaka area, and thus its products would have been transported overland.

31. Tarō puns on *kami*, "paper" and "god." Again, liberties have been taken in order to create an English-language pun.

32. Tarō's response puns on *kotowari*, "reason" or "excuse" and "to break a koto."

33. The exact significance of this name is unclear. *Uta* may refer to the Music Bureau, but there was no such position within the Music Bureau heirarchy. It probably refers to poetry in general, in which case Tarō's new name is equivalent to "Master Poet."

34. Emperor Ninmei (810–850) had many sons, some of whom succeeded to the throne, but it is unknown whether the exile in question was an actual historical figure.

35. Odaka could refer to either the Otaga or the Hotaka shrines, both in Nagano Prefecture.

36. This might also be read "Asahi."

37. Reigned 850–858.

38. *Honji*, translated here as "origins," refers to the origins of a god; the application of the term to a common person is highly unusual.

39. In syncretic Buddhism, the Three Heats *(sannetsu)* are torments that gods of the earth must undergo.

40. The relation of this line to the preceding lines is unclear.

The Errand Woman

Oyō no ama

In many respects, *The Errand Woman* is similar to the modern short story in its careful plotting and artful narration. This highly sophisticated story of a monk's capitulation to the attractions of the world he had renounced is similar to several setsuwa telling of lustful priests and to certain comic plays (kyōgen) poking fun at worldly mountain priests *(yamabushi)*. Unlike the rollicking burlesque of kyōgen, however, this tale is dry and ironic, recounted in a distanced, deadpan tone by a nonintrusive narrative persona. The errand woman is depicted as a clever catalyst who subtly leads the monk to forbidden shores while constantly assuring him of the purity of his motives. In this way, she allows him to rationalize each step of his growing commitment to the life of the flesh and thus seal his own fate. The negotiations through which this end is accomplished are highly poetic and refined, disguising their real purpose and implications.

I have translated the title of the story as "errand woman," although it might also be rendered "useful nun." During the medieval period, the term *ama* (nun) came to be used quite loosely to designate a range of single women, from ordained, tonsured nuns to itinerant proselytizers and even prostitutes. The woman described in the story appears to be similar to the *suai onna*, a trader of dry goods and clothing who sometimes engaged in prostitution.

This translation is based on the illustrated booklet (Nara ehon) housed in the Tokyo University Library Annex, annotated by Ichiko Teiji and printed in *Otogi-zōshi, kanazōshi*, ed. Ichiko Teiji and Noma Kōshin, Kanshō Nihon koten bungaku 26 (Tokyo: Kadokawa shoten, 1976), pp. 51–93. The illustrations, from the same source, have been provided courtesy of the Tokyo University Library. For the extremely unclear final line of the text, I have substituted the ending of a variant, and possibly earlier, *Errand Woman* illustrated scroll, which features a similar story with only slightly different wording except at the conclusion. This text may be found reproduced without annotations in *Otogi-zōshi emaki*, ed. Okudaira Hideo (Tokyo: Kadokawa shoten, 1982).

Near the Shirakawa[1] River in the capital area lived a monk who had renounced the world and constructed a small hut, existing so humbly that he could barely count on a steady supply of brushwood with which to cook his morning gruel. All day long he would sit behind his thatched door, beating on a small gong and reciting his prayers. One day an old woman bearing a bundle on her head came by.

"Is there anything you need. I'll take whatever you have—your used clothing, old silks, robes, underrobes, faded singlets, pieces of old scarves, scraps of old clerical neckbands, remnants of towels— and swap them for whatever you need." She sat down on the stoop, put aside her bundle, breathed a sigh of relief, and settled down to relax. "Well, well, you certainly are commendable, living all by yourself in such a place, saying your prayers. How admirable!"

The monk looked at her. "Where did you come from? You must have quite a few things in that bundle. At your age it must be difficult to carry so much around. Have some tea, and rest a while."

"I don't live anywhere in particular. I'm at home in all sorts of places here and there in the capital: in the palaces of the lords of Ichijō and Nijō or the regent Konoe,[2] in the halls of aristocrats and rooms of the imperial palace itself, in noble retreats, mansions of great lords, lodgings of their personal retainers, in all the branches

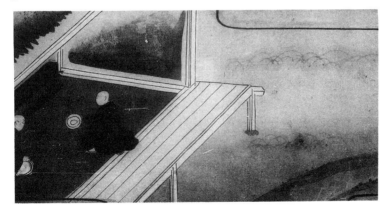

of the Gozan temple complex[3] and places of worship everywhere, in rooms of prostitutes and streetwalkers throughout the city, homes of townsmen and gentry alike, teahouses and wine merchants, diviner's shacks and cloth-stretching shops. I make my rounds everywhere, trading old cottons, used robes, torn scarves, scraps of cloth, worn sashes, old thread, silk remnants, combs, tweezers, sewing hooks, old powder and broken cosmetic dishes, shreds of tissue, even worn-out eyebrow brushes—for better things. I can get all kinds of things for you whenever you need them: poison antidotes, herbal remedies, panaceas, elixirs, ointments, eye balms, aloes, salves, fragrant compounds, sewing kits, paper fans, hairpins, and sword fastenings.

"What's more, I am in the confidence of those of good breeding: noble wives, court ladies, young novices, nuns, and ladies with no one else to guide them. If a gentleman has taken a fancy to any of them, I steer the course of his messages. If a lady's heart secretly yearns for another, I arrange a tryst, even to the depths of Longing Mountain. If she is anxious to avoid prying eyes and needs to know where her waves of passion may safely meet the waiting shore of her lover's arms, I arrange an encounter under the guise of a blossom- or moon-viewing excursion to Gion, Kiyomizu, or Kitano.[4] No one is the wiser, and eventually all my clients are joined together like twisted threads. I am at their bidding even in such trifling matters as these, and that is why they call me the errand woman. I am well known throughout the capital."

As she spoke, the monk became flustered and lost his place in his devotions.

"Well, you certainly are someone special, living alone in a place like this and saying your prayers. I really do admire you," she added.

"Hail to the Original Vow of the Blessed Buddha," he intoned, ringing the gong. But his interest had been snared. "Since I must live in this sad world—may the gods and buddhas forgive me—would you arrange for me to meet a lady of deep sensitivity, just this once, reverend nun?"

"Well, well! How sad! From the looks of things, you're well along in years, and likely to live alone here forever. Your nights must be very lonely! Indeed, even a young man would find the uncertainty of life here difficult to bear. How much worse for you at your age, with no one to care for you if you fall ill! You should want for nothing as you anticipate your future salvation." She spoke with deep sympathy.

"Yes, I agree, but I have no devoted disciples to rely on. Even I have found this to be a lonely, humble life that would wear hard on anyone unaccustomed to such unpleasant surroundings. I donned these monk's robes because I disliked the secular life, and I wouldn't want anyone to come to depend on me. I place my trust wholly in the vow of the Savior Buddha and calmly await the autumn winds beckoning from the west, when I shall vanish like a drop of dew."

"That is certainly commendable. Indeed, without a single disciple here, a novice might be uncomfortable. Although you have relinquished the self and entered the Path, as long as your fragile life continues you cannot do as you please. Even your simple robes of moss and sleeves of grass[5] become drenched with dew and touched by frost—they can't go without laundering! People like me—or even those with plenty of help—do get dirty over time. If only you had some well-intentioned person around! Why, even in this miserable hut, she could do chores like picking the vegetables, drawing the water, and chopping the kindling.[6] You could have your clothing mended and enjoy a massage whenever you're feeling under the weather. All you have to do is find the right person," she urged.

As he listened, the monk's resolve suddenly melted. "You're right: I am old and cannot count on living through the morrow. I would like someone tenderly to assist me in my twilight years. As long as my ephemeral existence continues, though it may hang by a fragile thread, it would be nice to have someone to do my washing and restitch my robes from time to time. They say that one needs a companion when crossing rough waters. Do what you must, go where you must, but find someone for me!" he begged.

"Well, as I've already said, I make my way around being useful to people. From the first moment I set eyes on you, for some reason I was moved by your plight. I've been wondering where I might

find just the right person to suit your needs. There's no one in the capital who might be appropriate. . . . I suppose I'll have to scour the countryside," she said, and made ready to depart. The monk followed her to the garden.

"I'm counting on you. I know that this is putting you to a great deal of trouble, but please make your inquiries quickly." Perhaps intending to speed matters, he pulled out a fan from his robe. "Wait a minute! Let me give you something. When you have the good fortune to find someone, give her this as a token of the time when she and I shall meet."[7]

"This is a most unexpected gift, but I'll accept it. When you are matched up with a good, faithful wife, your prosperity will expand just like the folds of this fan" They hurried through their leave-taking. "This is without doubt an auspicious omen. May it bring good luck," she said in parting.

Four or five days later the errand woman returned. "Well, I just don't know where I'm going to find the right woman. I've looked everywhere, and there was no one to be found. Those women I thought might fit the bill turned out to be either ugly, with drooping eyes, or old, with pursed lips."

The monk was desolate. "That's terrible! All my hopes have come to nothing! I was carried away by your words and asked for too much. All right, then, in that case good looks or youth isn't necessary. As long as she's suitable for me, why don't you just decide that I'll take her?" he said reproachfully.

"Just wait a moment and listen to me. Hidden away in seclusion near Yamazaki there lives a nun. People say that she used to live in the capital and that she is a daughter of an aristocrat. She has pleasant looks and a placid disposition, but her circumstances have changed, and she is desolate as drifting sea grass with no one to cling to. She has become a nun and lives in a poor shack. I found someone to approach her and test the waters, gently suggesting your invitation as delicately as the rustle of ripened heads of rice, but her heart was moved not at all. Perhaps had I urged her more strongly, tugging at her heartstrings as an archer would a bow, she might have relented. But then I wondered if the winds here had already shifted and were no longer blowing as ardently. That's why I came back here first."

"Wonderful!" said the monk. "If she is a person of such determination, now she may send a bitter harvest of nays downstream, but in the end she's bound to flow my way. Once she is won over to coming to a place like this and our love becomes as endless as the turns of a spool of yarn, why should she then have a change of heart? Quickly, go back and speak with her. I wonder how old she is?"

"How old? I couldn't go so far as to ask her age! But how old are you, reverend monk?"

"I'm not quite forty. I have suffered great hardships living in these conditions and consequently have become haggard. I probably appear over sixty," he replied, hedging the question.

"It is certainly true that those who suffer age beyond their natural years. Why, I myself am just past thirty. With the whole world my home and no place to rest my head, I have aged more than I should—I must look like an old woman! Even the great god of Kitano himself went completely white overnight.[8] If you are not yet forty, there's only a ten year difference. She's the right age and seems to be a good match for you. I'll do my best." She arose to take her leave.

"There's no need to consult with diviners or anyone like that about the match.[9] Just hurry and fix me up with someone good," he added as she left.

From that moment on, the monk eagerly awaited news. He was

uneasy and preoccupied, wondering when he would hear a positive response. After almost two months had passed without any word, he became increasingly discouraged and began to wonder if the old woman's story had been all a pack of lies. "Why did I pile up my hopes as high as Sayanonaka Mountain? If she only knew that my yearning for her is as deep as the evening mist rising from Muro-noyato Pond, she would not string me along like a boat tethered at Sano crossing. I shall call on her now and reveal my ripened love, as full as the reed plumes at Naniwa," he thought to himself. But, just as he had asked directions to the place called Yamazaki and was about to set out in a daze, the errand woman arrived.

"I'm so glad you're finally here! How did it go?" he asked.

"I know that I should have gotten back to you sooner, but various matters came up. I had to consult with people here and there and was detained until now. I'm sorry to have kept you waiting, but it really won't do to rush things like this. The lady is as hard to move as stone and her heart as difficult to pull as crumbling timber. I tried every possible means of persuasion, but, after all, she's like a fisherwoman in a drifting boat with no safe harbor. She thinks that she might bend to the breeze that so beckons, if only she could be assured of its constancy. 'Tell him,' she said, 'that the hearts of men these days are as unpredictable as the shallows and depths of a stream. If I became as accustomed to him as a well-worn oar to water and he were the kind of man who, like the shifting flow of the Asuka River, changes his heart from day to day, then my sleeves would be wet with tears. If he will vow fidelity to the end and never allow his regard to alter, no matter what the circumstances, I shall comply with his wishes.' "

"Well," replied the monk. "That's a simple matter. I am no callow youth of fickle heart. Hear me, oh gods of Tadasu Woods! Ye who examine all lies! I shall be ever faithful!"[10]

"Now there should be no trouble. I'll tell her of your vow. When would you like her to come?"

"It doesn't matter when—as soon as possible. Quickly!"

"I'll be back in two or three days without fail," she said, and left.

The only thing that dampened the spirits of the delighted monk was having to wait. As he counted the days, he was not himself; sleeping and waking, he lived in a dream. Hoping that he might first see her in his dreams, he would lift his head from the pillow and recite:

Yume ka to yo
mishi omokage mo
chigiri shi
utsutsu naraneba
wasurane. . . .

Was it then a dream?
I pledged love to a vision,
yet 'tis not real.
I cannot forget. . . .[11]

When the long-awaited day finally arrived, the monk weeded the garden. As he swept up the dust with his broom, he mused to himself that, when they plighted their troth, the sweep of his life-span might thereby be lengthened. He beat the mats and shook them out, then lined them neatly together; he shook out the bedding and spread it fastidiously, even down to the old pillow, and burned the trash, putting everything in perfect order. He even prepared various delicacies to eat and set them out in pleasing array. He cut kindling and heated water for tea in a kettle with a cracked lid, measured out some tea leaves, washed his battered cups, and set them on an old chipped tray. Then he waited, anticipating her imminent arrival.

Soon night fell, and the pine embers on the torch glowed faintly. He opened the door and stood gazing out. The clover rustling in the garden momentarily startled him into thinking that she had arrived, and in the murmuring leaves he heard her approaching footsteps. With pounding heart he waited through the dusk and into the light of the rising moon. "For whom do these sleeves glitter in the moonlight?" he wept, almost feeling betrayed. Soon the moon clouded over, and he could distinguish nothing in the darkness.

"I've exhausted myself weeding and sweeping the garden. Perhaps a bit of song will relax me," he thought, and sang:

By the veranda, the ever-clear white blossoms;
by the fence, a blanket of snow appears.
Even the glistening pine needles
appear to be the unfallen snow;
chrysanthemums remain in wintry fields,
they too look like fresh snow:
delightful, yet touched
with the sadness of a lonely mountain path.
By night, hearts are easily drawn together;
by day, the eyes of the world are watching. . . .[12]

As he was passing the time this way, there came the sounds of eager footsteps and a faint tapping at the door. His heart in his mouth, he arose and went out to find the errand woman on his doorstep.

"Well? How did it go?" he asked anxiously.

"Lower your voice! She's not used to this sort of thing! She was terribly shy, but at last I convinced her to come along. It won't do to have the lamp burning too brightly. Dim the lights everywhere and go inside quietly. I'll just slip her in and be on my way."

"Of course. She's young and inexperienced, and it's only natural for her to be shy. I'll put out the light. But, since you're leaving so soon, won't you first have a drink in honor of the occasion?"

"I shouldn't keep her waiting all alone, but perhaps I could celebrate just for a moment," she replied.

Somehow the monk had managed to procure some first-rate sake, which he now produced and served in a teacup. "Just a quick nip while we stand here," he said.

"That's no way to treat such good sake! It should be the other way around!" she said, taking hold of the flask.[13] Although he protested that he wanted only a sip, she urged him to drink more, pouring out a large quantity and replenishing the flask.

"Now it's my turn," she said, taking the cup and draining it several times. "Now it's your turn again," and she poured out more. After he had downed many cups in rapid succession, she said, "It's very late. After I bring her in, you won't need to drink any more. Drink now to your heart's content, then go to bed. At times like this, you can indulge as much as you like. After all, we're celebrating!" She pressed more and more on him, and soon he became quite besotted, completely losing track of how much he had consumed.

"I must bring her in now. Quickly, smother the lamp!" She left, but returned to add, "Behave yourself, and no rough language. Go to bed quietly."

"I quite understand." The monk's joy knew no bounds. He remained very still, and, after a while, he perceived that she had let the lady in. By raising the lampwick a bit, he was able to discern a figure wearing what seemed to be a gauze head covering, balancing something white atop her head, leaning on a large bundle, her face cast down demurely.

It seemed rude not to offer her at least something to drink. He raised the wick still further and brought out the tray with food and cups. When he pushed the flask toward her, she modestly drew her scarf closer, hiding her face in shadows.

"Of course, you're young and afraid of an old monk like me, but once I too was a young and vigorous peak of manhood. Now, now, it's late, and we must take shelter in the darkness of the mountain." He dimmed the lamp and picked up the cups. "Why are you so shy? You may be a fisherwoman on the shore, inexperienced with the waves of the deep, but if we are to harvest the sea grass of love, you must release your vessel from its mooring and take a sip."

Hesitantly, she put out her hand and drank. Although he could not distinguish reality in the darkness, he offered her more, and she drained the cup.

"Please have just a little more in honor of the occasion," he said, filling the cup once again. "Here, try some of this. Everything came up so suddenly that I have little to offer you." He urged her to eat some food and again poured out a brimming cupful of sake. "Now it's very late. Just one more."

Now the monk took the cup. "With this cup I celebrate a most joyous occasion!" he announced, drinking down several cups in a row. "This is wonderful! This joy come to me so late in life will grow ever greater!" He drank cup after cup, singing, "You are like the sliver of moon on the third of the second month; as much as I gaze, you appear only tonight.[14] Have some more to eat, drink as much as you like, and soon we'll go to bed."

"I've already had so much it's embarrassing! Please, reverend monk, eat and drink more than your custom. Sake is a good tonic for your virility. Drink it up."

Thus it grew later and later. He drained the cup and set it down by the hot water, made some tea, drank a few sips, then set it aside hastily and extinguished the lamp.

"The consort Yu wept a river of tears, yet her bedchamber must have been like this one tonight,"[15] he remarked flatteringly. "Good night." He lay down beside her. "Well, I never thought it possible that someone like you would come here—to this thatched hut, drenched with dew, where deer sleep and quail nest, a place even I regard as a great hardship." He inched closer.

"That errand woman, or whatever she's called," replied his companion, "tried one argument after another, as incessantly as the beating wings of a snipe, as varied as the colors of autumn grass, but I thought that, if a man's heart is indeed like a flower, then it too might wither. I could not bear the sorrow if, like the fickle autumn rains, you were to drench me with love, only suddenly to cease. Thus, harbored at the port of Nays, I rejected your offer. But your vow of fidelity, sworn to the gods of Tadasu Woods, made me feel that I could trust you. So shyly I set out under the leaves of

Modest Woods and now meet you for the first time." She spoke in a modest tone, shyly and delicately shielding her face.

"Why indeed should my heart be like the short-lived blossoms of spring? When I was a young blade thrusting through the snow, I may have been fickle, but now the dews of age from Ancient Woods have fallen on me, and I no longer feel the maple-scarlet passions tossed hither and yon by autumn winds. May my pledge be as true and constant as the evergreens of Eternal Mountain! I am old, yet you regard my affection as the fleeting dews of youth. Don't be as distant as the far-off plains! Nestle by me, and we shall be as close as brush in a field. Even a wild pony taken from its pasture grows accustomed to a new master. Let us converse together and exchange intimacies, drinking the dewy elixir of fulfillment. The senses are beguiled in the fullness of this night. Let us lie down together and vow that the current of our love shall surround us, running deep and true. Even if we made a thousand nights into one, it would still be too brief. Let us be husband and wife."

"Oh, how thrilling! Words just can't describe it!"

"I quite forgot—you've come all the way from Yamazaki and must be exhausted. Shall I massage your feet? Why don't you take off your underrobe? Might I ask your age?"

They were still immersed in pillow talk when the tolling of the morning bell and the crowing of the cock signaled the break of day. Sunlight gradually seeped through the crannies in the walls, and, as the room grew brighter, the monk realized that their scattered robes had become chilled. It was time to rise. As he pushed open the side door, he caught a clear glimpse of her face: she was an old crone of at least seventy, with a wrinkle-seamed face and nary a tooth left in her mouth. He stared in disbelief, unable to take his eyes off her.

"How can you stare at me so idiotically? How mortifying!" She arose, tidied her robes and adjusted her scarf, then sat down and leaned against her bundle with a purposeful air, keeping her face averted. The monk examined her closely: it was the old errand woman herself. Speechless with shock, he could only gape foolishly.

"That Yamazaki woman that I mentioned—well, I did speak

with her, but my words piled up to no avail like dry leaves. Nothing I said moved her in the least, so I came back here and told you about it. But you reproached me, saying, 'Why don't you just go ahead and invite anyone? What a shame! How terrible!' Well, there simply was no one else to be found, but I couldn't disappoint you. So off I went again, wondering what to do. If you felt that strongly, then even someone like myself could serve to ease your burden. I could do loads of laundry and massage your back. But then I realized that you might react just as you do now, and, if you did, this old cast-off fisherwoman's boat would be soaked in the bitter brine of resentment. I pondered your intentions well, and, since you took that binding oath, I figured that everything would be all right. Have you forgotten your own vow? Our ages are probably no more than a year apart. Isn't it a perfect match?

"And what's more—it may seem funny—but let me give you a rough idea of what I have in this bag here. Torn robes, old silk scarves, a tattered court hat, a bleached out skirt, a scrap of sash, patched leggings, an old gauntlet, a face towel, a paring knife, some hemp that, given thread, could be stitched together, white linen, skeins of hemp, Chinese crimson, an eyeless needle, mirror fragments, a nail parer, and kettle rings.

"As I look around at your things, I see only dirty bedclothes, torn bedding, an old hood, a tattered sash, an old hand towel, a chipped tea kettle, a cracked tea bowl, a bamboo tea measure, a bamboo ladle, a shallow cooking pot with only stones for support, a bucket with broken hoops, a sake flask with the handle knocked off, an old floor mat, torn straw matting, and a rush blind. If we put our things together, we'll live easily and want for nothing. As we live together and drink from the same stream, it wouldn't be quite honest to act like pious novices! But, if we say our prayers devoutly and call on the Savior Buddha, there is no reason why we can't achieve salvation. You know that there are four kinds of believers;[16] you don't need to practice monkish austerities, merely to be sincere at heart."

The dazed monk sat speechless. "Well, this too might be the seed of enlightenment, if I but say my prayers in all sincerity," he mused.

"And, with my voice added to yours, why shouldn't we be reborn together in the Pure Land?" she concluded.[17]

NOTES

1. In the northeast of present-day Kyoto.

2. Ichijō, Nijō, and Konoe refer to three of a group of high-ranking families known as the *gosekke*, from which the regent and chancellor were selected.

3. The five great Zen temples in the hills outside Kyoto.

4. These three religious centers were extremely popular in the medieval period as pilgrimage and trysting sites.

5. A common epithet for clerical robes.

6. Practical austerities of the ascetic life. Ideally, one should perform these humble chores for himself in order to cultivate a proper frame of mind.

7. The monk is employing a common pun: *ōgi* (fan) is homophonous with *augi* (encounter). The fan also plays a part in *yuino*, a betrothal ceremony in which the prospective mates exchange tokens.

8. A reference to Sugawara no Michizane, a scholar and statesman exiled to Kyushu and later deified. In the otogi-zōshi *Tenjin*, it is stated that hardship turned his hair white overnight.

9. It was customary to consult diviners about the auspiciousness and appropriateness of prospective matches.

10. The Tadasu Woods *(Tadasu no mori)* is at the junction of the Kamo and Takano rivers in Kyoto, at the site of the Shimogamo shrine. The god

of Tadasu, Taketsunami no mikoto, is said to have presided at the first court hearing.

11. Owing to the poor condition of the manuscript, this verse has several elisions. It appears to be a misquotation of or allusion to *Shinkokinshū* no. 1390: "Yume ka to yo / mishi omokage mo / chigirishi mo / wasurezu nagara / utsutsu naraneba" (Was it then a dream? / I cannot forget / the figure I saw / the vows we swore / but reality betrays this).

12. The monk's song is a poetic pastiche centering around mistaking various phenomena for snow, homophonous with the verb *yuki*, "to go." This may have been a contemporary song, but the source is unknown. The final two lines, also seen in *Lazy Tarō,* closely resemble *Kanginshū* no. 256: "Hito no kokoro to / Katada no ami to wa / yoru koso hikiyokere / yoru koso yokere / hiru wa hitome no / shigekereba" (His heart and a Katada net / must be pulled at night / night is the best / for during the day / eyes press in closely).

13. Marriage customs dictate that the groom drink the ceremonial sake first, followed by the bride. Here, the monk assumes that the errand woman is acting as a proxy for the woman she has escorted.

14. The monk is likening the woman's elusiveness to that of the new moon.

15. An allusion, well known to contemporary Japanese, to Hsiang Yü and his beloved consort Yü, who shared wine on the eve of his certain defeat.

16. Monks, nuns, laymen, and laywomen.

17. The portion beginning with "If we say our prayers devoutly . . ." to the end has been borrowed from the version of the story printed in *Otogi-zōshi emaki.* The last two lines given here are picture captions. I have deleted the last line of the *Otogi-zōshi, Kana-zōshi* text, which reads: "At the time I left Kenchō Temple, I realized that it is hard to part with even a pillar in the corner of the hall, once one has grown used to it." This seems to mean that the woman believes the monk will learn to accept and even grow fond of the new domestic arrangement he has unwittingly contracted.

Suggested English-Language Readings

Araki, James. "Bunshō Sōshi: The Tale of Bunshō, the Saltmaker." *Monumenta Nipponica* 38:3 (1983).

———. "Otogi-zōshi and Nara ehon: A Field of Study in Flux." *Monumenta Nipponica* 36:1 (1981).

Childs, Margaret. "Chigo monogatari: Love Stories or Buddhist Sermons." *Monumenta Nipponica* 35:2 (1980).

Dykstra, Yoshiko K. *Miraculous Tales of the Lotus Sutra from Ancient Japan: The Dainihonkoku Hokekyōkenki of Priest Chingen.* Honolulu: University of Hawaii Press, 1983.

Elison, George, and Bardwell Smith, eds. *Warlords, Artisans, and Commoners: Japan in the Sixteenth Century.* Honolulu: University of Hawaii Press, 1981.

Geddes, Ward. *Kara Monogatari: Tales of China.* Occasional Paper no. 16. Arizona State University, Center for Asian Studies, 1984.

Kavanaugh, Frederick. "Twenty Representative Muromachi Period Prose Narratives: An Analytic Study." Ph.D. diss., University of Hawaii, 1985.

Matisoff, Susan. *The Legend of Semimaru, Blind Musician of Japan.* New York: Columbia University Press, 1973.

Mills, Douglas E. *A Collection of Tales from Uji: A Study and Translation of Uji Shūi Monogatari.* Cambridge: Cambridge University Press, 1970.

———. "Medieval Japanese Tales, Part II." *Folklore* 84 (1973).

———. "The Tale of the Mouse: Nezumi no sōshi." *Monumenta Nipponica* 34:2 (1979).

Morrell, Robert E. *Sand and Pebbles (Shasekishū).* Albany: State University of New York Press, 1985.

Mulhearn, Chieko Irie. "Cinderella and the Jesuits: An Otogizōshi Cycle as Christian Literature." *Monumenta Nipponica* 34:4 (1979).

———. "Otogi-zōshi: Short Stories of the Muromachi Period." *Monumenta Nipponica* 29:2 (1974).

Nakamura, Kyoko Motomichi. *Miraculous Stories from the Japanese Buddhist Tradition: The Nihon Ryōiki of the Monk Kyōkai.* Cambridge, Mass.: Harvard University Press, 1973.

Putzar, Edward. "The Tale of Monkey Genji: Sarugenji-zōshi." *Monumenta Nipponica* 18:1 (1963).

Ruch, Barbara. "Medieval Jongleurs and the Making of a National Literature." In *Japan in the Muromachi Age,* ed. John W. Hall and Toyoda Takeshi. Berkeley: University of California Press, 1977.

————. "Origins of the Companion Library: An Anthology of Medieval Japanese Stories." *Journal of Asian Studies* 30:3 (1971).

————. "The Other Side of Culture in Medieval Japan." In *The Cambridge History of Japan.* Vol. 3, *Medieval Japan,* ed. Kozo Yamamura. Cambridge: Cambridge University Press, 1990.

————. " 'Otogi-bunko' and Short Stories of the Muromachi Period." Ph.D. diss., Columbia University, 1965.

Skord, Virginia. "The Comic Consciousness in Medieval Japanese Narrative: Otogi-zōshi of Commoners." Ph.D. diss., Cornell University, 1987.

————. "From Rags to Riches and Beyond: Monogusa Tarō." *Monumenta Nipponica* 44:2 (1989).

Steven, Chigusa. "Hachikazuki: A Muromachi Short Story." *Monumenta Nipponica* 32:3 (1977).

Tyler, Royall. *Japanese Tales.* New York: Pantheon, 1987.

————. *The Miracles of the Kasuga Deity.* New York: Columbia University Press, 1990.

Ury, Marian. *Tales of Times Now Past: Sixty-two Stories from a Medieval Japanese Collection.* Berkeley: University of California Press, 1979.

About the Author

Virginia Skord received her doctorate from Cornell University. She is currently assistant professor of Asian Studies at Manhattanville College, where she teaches Japanese language and literature. Her major fields of interest include medieval Japanese narrative, the interplay of text and illustration, and the conventions of humorous expression.

Production Notes
This book was designed by Roger Eggers.
Composition and paging were done on the
Quadex Composing System and typesetting
on the Compugraphic 8400 by the design
and production staff of University of
Hawaii Press.
The text typeface is Garamond and the
display typeface is ITC Garamond.
Offset presswork and binding were done by
The Maple-Vail Book Manufacturing Group.
Text paper is Glatfelter Offset Vellum,
basis 50.